By **BENJAMIN FLINDERS**

Illustrations by NICOLAUS SERR

FLINDERS PRESS

www.flinderspress.com

For Analee, who shares Leeana's face; and Kennady, who shares her character. And for Nate and Chad, who taught Ethan and Dallin how to shoot slingshots, bows and arrows long before they went to Camelot.

Traveling Trunk Adventures #3: Excalibur

Text copyright © 2011 by Benjamin Flinders
Illustrations copyright © 2011 by Flinders Press
All rights reserved. Published by Flinders Press, Inc.

Library of Congress Control Number: 2010931661
ISBN: 978-0-9843955-6-9

Printed in China

CONTENTS

Prologue

One week ago, Ethan and Dallin received a mysterious, old-fashioned trunk from their dad. The brothers quickly discovered that the enchanted chest, which they nicknamed the traveling trunk, could take them anywhere throughout history.

On their first accidental adventure, they found themselves aboard a pirate ship in the New World. Five days later they climbed out of a trunk of whale vomit into the ancient city of Atlantis before it was lost forever in the depths of the sea.

The traveling trunk is a portal to excitement and adventure that has the two brothers at odds. Dallin can't wait for the next adventure to begin and checks the trunk several times a day. Ethan dreads the day when the toys in the trunk will vanish, to be replaced with clothing for whatever time in history they are about to travel to.

Much to Dallin's excitement, the trunk just delivered black tunics embroidered with a red-winged snake coiled around a sword.

CHAPTER 1

Armory

Lifting the trunk lid, Ethan and Dallin shielded their eyes. Morning sunlight poured through several windows set in thick stone walls, glinting off of shiny metal.

Climbing out of the traveling trunk, Dallin shouldered his old school backpack filled with emergency supplies and looked around. "Wow! What is this place?"

Colorful tapestries, swords, shields, bows and other weapons adorned the walls. Suits of armor and chain mail stood at attention in rows, like a squad of soldiers awaiting orders. The room glowed with reflected sunlight as it bounced off all the polished steel.

"This looks like an armory," Ethan said, closing the trunk lid. Noticing his brother's confused look he

added, "It's where knights store their weapons when they're not using them."

"Knights must be really strong," Dallin grunted, lifting a heavy metal helmet onto his head. "How can they see in this thing?"

Ethan perused the stockpile of weapons and armor. "This is pretty cool. Maybe this adventure won't be as dangerous as the last two, and we can just take a quick look around and then head back home."

Numerous swords of various shapes and sizes lined the walls. Ethan grabbed the biggest weapon—a greatsword—from off a mount and examined the blade. It was a lot sharper and heavier than the cutlasses they had used on their first adventure with the pirates. Grasping the ornate handle with two hands, he swung it through the air like a baseball bat. The greatsword threw him off balance and it slipped from his hands, falling to the floor with an ear-splitting clang. The sound of metal colliding with stone rang throughout the armory, echoing off the walls.

"Uh oh," Dallin said. Normally he was the one who got them into trouble.

"Sorry," Ethan mumbled. As he reached for the

weapon, the wooden door at the far end of the room rattled.

"Quick, hide!" Ethan said. Abandoning the greatsword, he pushed Dallin behind a pile of horse armor.

The heavy door creaked open, revealing a tall, slender girl dressed in a flowing blue gown. Her hazel eyes, angular chin and smooth olive complexion were framed by silky brown hair that cascaded off her shoulders like melted chocolate. Her bangs were braided around her head like a tiara.

"Who goes there?" she asked, glancing around the armory. Her eyes stopped on the fallen sword. She scanned the room one more time before walking in.

"She's pretty," Ethan thought out loud. "I wonder if she is a princess."

"Since you're so interested, why don't you go talk to her?" Dallin whispered.

"I am not," Ethan protested, shaking his head. "But maybe we should find out who she is."

"And where we are," Dallin added.

The girl placed the greatsword back in its mount on the wall and turned around to find the two brothers standing before her.

"Hi," Ethan said.

The girl jumped back in surprise, bracing herself against the wall.

"Real smooth with the introductions," Dallin teased.

The girl stared intently at their tunics, her eyes widening. Slowly, her hand began to creep along the wall.

"Sorry," Ethan said, holding up both hands in a gesture of peace. "We didn't mean to startle you; we just wanted to know—"

The girl didn't wait for Ethan to finish. Yanking the greatsword off the wall she lunged at them, swinging the blade in a wide arc.

Ethan and Dallin did the only natural thing to do; they screamed like little girls and jumped out of the way. Dallin somersaulted across the room, while Ethan flopped onto his belly and crawled for shelter.

"Yiaaa!" the girl yelled, chasing after Ethan and trapping him in front of the pile of horse armor. She hoisted the greatsword above her head and prepared to strike.

"Wait!" he yelled, throwing up his hands to shield himself. "We just want to ask you a question."

The girl hesitated for a second, but that was one

second too long. The greatsword proved too heavy, and she teetered backwards under the weight, slipping on her dress. To keep from falling over, she dropped the sword and wind-milled her arms for balance.

Ethan took advantage of the girl's distraction and jumped to his feet, advancing cautiously.

Regaining her composure, she twisted to face Ethan. Their eyes locked. They both looked down at the greatsword, and then back at each other. Ethan sprang for the weapon. Instead of fighting him for it, the girl ran to a row of smaller swords and detached one from the wall.

Not to be left out of the action, Dallin pried a scimitar from the hands of a dented suit of armor. He rotated his wrist, swinging the sword around in a circle like knights did in the movies, but then clumsily dropped the blade.

"Dallin! Stop goofing off and help me," Ethan shouted, taking a defensive stance behind the greatsword.

"She's just a girl," Dallin retorted. "This will be a piece of cake." Trying to sound heroic, he charged the girl, "Surrender fiend, or eat steel!"

The girl spun around with a broadsword in hand.

As the two blades collided Dallin almost dropped his scimitar a second time.

Metal clashed against metal as the two exchanged blows.

Dallin quickly realized that this girl was the better swordsman—or swords-girl in this case—and thought a quick surrender might be better for his health than a fight to the death. "I was just kidding about eating steel. Maybe we should call a truce?"

When the girl did not relent, Ethan jumped into the fray.

The brothers traded blows with the girl, but she proved to be a much fiercer fighter than they had expected—for a girl.

Her blocks, parries and stabs were far superior to theirs, but since it was two against one, the boys pressed their advantage.

"We are *not*...trying...to hurt you!" Ethan grunted between clangs.

"Then why have ye broken into my house?" she demanded.

Dallin's hands were beginning to go numb from the vibrations of the clanging blades. With a powerful thrust-and-twist combo, the girl knocked the scimitar from his hands, forcing him out of the fight. Narrowing her eyes, she focused on Ethan.

"We are here to help!" Ethan yelped, jumping over the girl's broadsword as it swept under his feet.

"Liar!" she screamed, thrusting and spinning like a ballet dancer, all the while backing Ethan into a corner.

The heavy greatsword was beginning to slip from Ethan's sweaty palms.

Spinning, the girl swung her broadsword with both hands. The powerful blow knocked Ethan's weapon from his grip, and it flipped end over end through the air before clattering to the ground.

"Now ye shall taste the wrath of House Lancelot," the girl cried, raising her sword for the final blow.

CHAPTER 2

A Coat for Arms

Whoosh!

A small stone shot across the room, striking the girl's raised sword arm.

"Ow!" she cried out in pain, losing her grip on the broadsword.

Ethan lunged at the unarmed girl, tackling her to the ground. "Stop fighting! We don't want to hurt you!" he blurted.

Her hazel eyes glowed with fury, and she clawed like a wild cat. Ethan barely managed to keep her fingers and nails away from his face.

"Stop! Don't make me shoot again!" Dallin yelled, pointing his reloaded slingshot at the girl. She stared at the unusual weapon and stopped struggling. Ethan released her, and stood up.

"That's better," he sighed, catching his breath.

"Nice shot, Dallin. That was quick thinking."

Dallin was a sharp-shooter with his slingshot. Before his family moved into their condominium in Los Angeles, he used to sit in his backyard in Virginia and shoot leaves off the hickory trees. On a good day, Dallin could hit one of those spiky green caterpillars, a hickory horned devil, off a leaf fifty feet away.

"It's a good thing we put together an emergency kit," Dallin said.

After their fist two adventures, Ethan decided they needed to be better prepared if they were going to do any more traveling. Dallin found an old backpack, and the brothers loaded it with supplies, which included Dallin's slingshot.

Nodding in agreement, Ethan said, "You can put the slingshot away now. I think she's ready to listen."

Dallin lowered his arm, tired from holding the elastic bands taut. He kept the rock in the slingshot's leather pocket just in case.

"I shall never listen to ye, nor anyone of Mordred House," the girl spat, sliding away from Ethan and Dallin, a mixture of fear and defiance in her eyes. She rubbed the back of her bruised hand, glaring with hatred at the emblem on their clothes: a red-winged

snake coiled around a sword.

"Look, we are not from around here," Ethan said.

"Wherever here is," Dallin shrugged, looking around.

"Ye lie," she scowled.

"What makes you think we are liars?" Ethan asked.

"Ye are wearing Mordred's coat of arms."

"I'm not wearing a coat on my arms," Dallin said, looking from his left arm to his right.

"She doesn't mean a jacket," Ethan sighed. Pointing to his tunic, he continued, "This snake and sword symbol must be the coat of arms for a knight named Mordred. All knights have their own coat of arms, or symbol. They put it on their armor, banners, and just about everything else. Since we are wearing these clothes, she must think we are his squires."

Ethan loved stories about knights, having read many books about them.

"What's a squire?" asked Dallin.

"Someone who works for a knight," Ethan answered. "In return for serving faithfully, the knight teaches his squires everything he knows."

"Really, like what kind of things?"

"Like jousting, sword fighting and horseback riding."

"Cool! I sure hope we get to do lots of horseback riding," Dallin said. "But who is this Mordred guy?"

Ethan shrugged. They both looked at the girl expectantly.

"He is the sworn enemy of King Arthur and all the Knights of the Square Table, which makes thee my enemy," Leeana spat.

"We are not your enemy. We've never even met Mordred—" Ethan stopped, his eyes widening. "Did you say *King Arthur*, as in *the* King Arthur of Camelot?"

Realizing where Ethan was going, Dallin said, "Ethan, didn't she say something about feeling the wrath of House Lancelot?"

"Whoa!" Ethan quickly put two and two together. "So, does that mean you are the daughter of Sir Lancelot, Knight of the Round Table?"

The girl did not answer. She just stared at the weapon still in Dallin's hand.

"Like I said," Ethan repeated, "We are not from around here. We were given these clothes in order to blend in. Besides, we've never even met Mordred. Don't you think that if Mordred sent us here to hurt you we would have done so already?"

Opening her mouth to protest, the girl realized Ethan might be speaking the truth.

"Look, we don't want to hurt you. We want to be your friend," Dallin said, returning the slingshot to his backpack.

Ethan extended a hand to help the girl off the ground.

She eyed him for a full minute before accepting. "Who are ye, truthfully?"

"I'm Ethan, and this is my brother Dallin."

"How did ye get into my father's armory?"

"Um, I don't think you would believe us if we told you," Ethan shrugged, looking at Dallin.

"Why? Because ye are spies?" she accused.

"No! Because we got here by magic," Dallin blurted out. When she did not seem surprised, he pointed at the large chest in the middle of the chamber and continued, "We climbed out of that trunk. We have a similar one back home. It gives us clothes for wherever the magic is going to take us, and then opens a doorway through another trunk, anywhere in the world. We never know exactly where..."

"Or when," Ethan added.

"...we are going to end up. Today we landed here in your armory."

The girl paused. Her eyes narrowed as she scrutinized their faces. She glanced at the armory door thinking, and then back at the boys. Slowly, a charming smile spread across her face.

"Well, why did ye not say so in the first place? I am Leeana, daughter of Sir Lancelot." She curtsied.

"What, just like that?" Ethan said in surprise. "One minute you think we are your sworn enemy, and the next you welcome us like best friends?"

"Of course. If magic sent thee to help me, then I have nothing to fear."

"But what if we lied?" Dallin said.

"But we didn't lie," Ethan said quickly, scowling at his brother. "Why are you trying to confuse the girl," he whispered. "You want her to attack us again?"

"I just thought she believed us too easily."

A shadow passed across Leeana's face, but then her radiant smile returned. "No, ye lie not. Indeed thou art sent by magic. Thy speech is different than mine, and ye have strange weapons which I have

17

never beheld. Furthermore, how else could ye have entered my father's locked armory? The fallen sword attracted my attention, but the door was locked before I did enter."

"Good, I am glad we got that all settled," Ethan sighed. He did not want to cross blades with this girl again.

"Me too," Dallin said. "Now, can you show us where the Knights of the Round Table hang out?"

Dong! Dong! Dong!

Bells chimed in the distance.

"Come, the tolling of the bells signify that King Arthur sitteth in judgment, and court will begin within the hour," Leeana said. "I don't know why, but my father said it is a matter of life and death that my family be there this day. Hurry, we must depart posthaste."

"You're going to take us to Camelot?" Dallin said.

Stopping at the armory exit, Leeana turned around and looked the boys over from head to toe. "Yes, but first we must get thee some cloaks; else ye shall be mistaken as Mordred's squires and thrown into the dungeon."

CHAPTER 3

Camelot

Having found suitable cloaks for Ethan and Dallin to cover their black tunics—and Dallin's backpack—Leeana led them to the stables. Three saddled horses stood ready.

"How did you know to have three horses waiting?" Ethan asked in surprise.

"Truthfully, I did not know that thou would be joining me," Leeana admitted. "But a young maiden cannot ride to the castle without escorts. My father's squires would have gone with me had thou not arrived."

Addressing one of the tall boys that stood waiting with the horses, Leeana said, "Bors, I am no longer in need of thine and thy brother's services. These new squires shall escort me."

"Yes, Mistress," Bors bowed, handing the reigns of a beautiful white mare to Leeana.

She sprang onto the horse's back as gracefully as a lioness leaping onto its prey.

Ethan and Dallin looked at each other, and then at their horses.

"This is so cool," Dallin said, staring up at the large black stallion in front of him. "We've never ridden a *real* horse before."

Turning her mare around to face the boys, Leeana said, "What dost thou mean when ye say ye have never ridden a *real* horse?"

"We have ridden on fake horses in carousels, but never on a real live one," Dallin explained, putting his foot in the stirrup and trying to pull himself up.

"Ye have never ridden a live horse, but ye have ridden *fake* horses?" Leeana gasped. "Truly, ye must be powerful magicians to be able to ride horses that are not real!"

"No, it's not like that," Ethan said, pulling himself up onto a massive brown charger. "The fake horses are run by electricity."

"Is 'Electricity' thy magician?" Leeana asked. "Our magician is named Merlin."

Ethan rolled his eyes.

"A little help here, please?" Dallin begged, still trying to mount his giant horse. Despite being the smallest of the three riders, he somehow managed to get the largest animal, and the stirrups were set too high to be of any use from the ground.

Bors and his brother watched, trying to stifle their laughter. After several failed attempts, they assisted by pushing Dallin all the way up. Finally seating himself in the saddle, Dallin was shocked to find that he was facing the rear of the horse instead of its head.

"Hey, how did the horse get turned around?"

The squires could not contain their amusement any longer, and they burst out laughing. Leeana did a better job of masking her smile.

After Dallin managed to turn himself around in the saddle, Leeana led them out of the stables and onto the main road leading to Camelot.

Riding through a cluster of cottages and scattered farms, they mounted a small hill. From this perspective, the boys beheld a marvelous sight laid out before them.

A majestic city of speckled white granite lay along the southern bank of a wide, meandering river.

Lofty spires and towers were strategically built around its perimeter. On the southern bank rolled vast golden fields of grain, rich patches of fruit orchards, and a smattering of livestock.

Rising from the middle of the city stood a small hill upon which sat the most magnificent castle Ethan and Dallin had ever seen, far surpassing the grandeur of any fairy tale picture book. Brightly colored stained-glass windows caught the morning sun, reflecting rays of red, blue and green. Regal purple flags fluttered from the castle ramparts, emblazoned with a golden lion rearing up on its hind legs.

"Cool," Dallin exhaled.

Leeana smiled warmly. "Welcome to Camelot."

"Amazing," Ethan said. "Never in my wildest dreams did I think that some day I would actually see the famous city of Camelot, home to King Arthur and the Knights of the Round Table."

"Ye mean Square Table," Leeana corrected.

"Huh?"

But before Ethan could get clarification, Leeana urged her horse faster, yelling over her shoulder, "Come, we must hurry or we shall miss the judgment."

Ethan saw Leeana lightly kick her heels into the horse's flanks, so he did the same. His horse galloped off after Leeana.

"Hey, wait for me," Dallin yelled as his brother and the girl took off without him. He did not see how they got their horses going so fast, and they did not hear his call over the clopping of their horses' hooves.

"Come on horsey, let's go," Dallin pleaded, patting the horse's neck.

His horse snorted loudly and continued its leisurely trot.

"I said let's go!" Dallin commanded, pulling on the reigns. But instead of going faster, pulling the reigns made the horse stop.

"Come on! We're going to get left behind!" Dallin pleaded, seeing his two companions getting farther and farther away.

The horse turned its head around slowly and looked at Dallin with large, dark eyes. Then it trotted over to the side of the road, lowered its head, and began munching on the tall grass.

"Aaagh!" Dallin yelled in frustration, slapping his hand down onto the horse's rump.

Neigh-he-he-he, the horse whinnied, rearing up on its hind legs.

Dallin grabbed onto the horse's mane to keep from sliding off, and screamed, "Yee-haw!"

The horse brought its front legs crashing back down to the earth and took off like an arrow shot from a bow. Dallin held on for dear life as the horse flew over the ground, quickly catching up to Ethan and Leeana long before they entered the city gate.

CHAPTER 4

The Square Table

Stabling their hoses outside the castle, Ethan and Dallin followed Leeana through the crowd toward the entrance. Even though the castle was in the middle of Camelot, and protected by the city's outer walls, a moat still surrounded the castle. The only way in or out was to go over the drawbridge.

As they crossed the moat, Dallin slowed down to glance over the edge, hoping to see alligators, piranhas or other ferocious creatures protecting the castle. The dark, murky water revealed nothing. The only life in the moat appeared to be along the marshy bank, where fat bullfrogs sunbathed on lily pads between thick clumps of cattails.

Turning to tell Ethan about the frogs, Dallin saw something move out of the corner of his eye. A large shadow stirred just below the surface, but before he could get a good look at it, the dark depths became unnaturally still.

Spooked by the shadow, Dallin leapt forward to catch up to his brother, crashing into an armed guard at the end of the drawbridge.

"Um, sorry," Dallin murmured as he backed up and moved around the intimidating figure.

A spear dug into the ground inches in front of Dallin's foot.

"Hey!" he blurted out, jumping back. "I'm walking here!"

"No children allowed inside the castle during Judgment," the guard boomed.

Hearing the commotion, Leeana returned to collect her escort. "This squire is with House Lancelot," she said.

The guard saluted. "My humble apologies, milady. Forgive me. I could not see thy family's coat of arms beneath the squire's cloak. Please proceed."

When the guard was far enough behind to not hear, Dallin whispered his thanks.

"Just stay close, and do not draw attention to thyself," Leeana instructed.

Entering the castle proper, they walked through an inner courtyard surrounded by manicured gardens and blossoming fruit trees. In the center of the courtyard stood a life-like statue of a young woman wrapped in a bejeweled shawl that sparkled in the morning sunlight. Passing more armored guards, they finally entered the Hall of Judgment.

Sunlight poured in through the open windows, and a cool breeze ruffled twelve flags mounted along the walls. Each flag bore a different coat of arms for King Arthur's choice knights, the Knights of the Square Table. A large purple banner with a gold lion hung from the highest rafter in the center of the room. The stone walls were adorned with tapestries depicting epic battles between men and foul beasts. Knights in shining armor slashed giants down to size, and dragons fell from the sky impaled by long lances. Most impressive of all was the central tapestry. It depicted a broad-shouldered man with a glowing blue sword standing atop a mountain of gruesome goblins, having defeating them in single combat.

Crowding the center of the spacious chamber sat a square table. At its head stood an ornate gold throne.

Leeana led them around the square table to crowded wooden benches lining the edges of the hall. She stopped in front of a beautiful woman holding a delicate handkerchief.

"Mother," Leeana curtsied. "This is Squire Ethan and Squire Dallin."

Ethan and Dallin bowed to the majestic lady.

Leeana's mother moved over to make room for her daughter. "Sit, daughter. The Judgment beginneth soon."

A rotund handmaid stood and moved behind Leeana's mother, allowing Ethan and Dallin to sit. Ethan smiled at her, and she smiled back.

Settling in next to Leeana, Ethan leaned over and whispered, "What's with the square table?"

Leeana raised an eyebrow. "What dost thou mean? What is wrong with a square table?"

"The table should be round."

"Why should it be—"

Trumpets blared from the back of the hall. Everyone jumped to their feet and ceased speaking as the fanfare began.

Ethan was glad they had front row seats when twelve armored men walked into the hall. As King

Arthur led the procession of knights, the morning sunlight reflected off his shiny armor, dazzling the crowd with its reflected radiance. The effect was magnificent. With the trumpets singing, and the sunlight dancing, it was as if the hosts of heaven had descended into the castle hall.

King Arthur stopped before the throne, waiting for the eleven knights to take their places in front of leather-cushioned seats that surrounded the square table. Arthur was tall and muscular, his tousled brown hair held in place by a band of gold that circled his forehead.

The seat immediately to the king's right remained vacant. Ethan turned to ask Leeana about it, but stopped when he saw her staring at the empty spot with a look of concern on her face.

The music abruptly ceased.

King Arthur pulled a beautifully adorned scabbard from his side and set it on the table, its point facing the middle. The scabbard should have contained a sword, but it was empty.

The king sat.

In unison, the remaining eleven men drew their swords. The air filled with the ringing sound of metal blades sliding out of scabbards.

Lifting their swords into the air, the knights pledged their allegiance:

> We pledge our honor and our swords;
> To be just and fair and honest Lords;
> Without pay or great rewards;
> Our bond is stronger than iron cords.
>
> We promote the code of chivalry;
> To be gallant warriors of courtesy;
> To be loved because of generosity;
> To uphold our king, his Majesty.

The knights plunked their swords on the table, tips pointing away from their chairs, and sat down as one. The people of Camelot followed suit, at least those that had benches to sit on.

King Arthur looked at the vacant seat to his right, ran his hands over his bearded face, then stood.

"Knights of the Square Table," the king's majestic voice boomed. "Today we shall pass judgment upon one of our own."

Signaling several guards standing at a rear passageway, King Arthur instructed, "Bring in the prisoner."

CHAPTER 5

Traitor to the Crown

Armored guards escorted in a dark-haired man bound in chains. Leeana gasped, and the crowd shifted nervously. Even the knights themselves could not hide their shock upon seeing the prisoner.

Several knights, as well as many in the audience, glanced in Ethan and Dallin's direction. But they were not looking at the boys; they were staring at Leeana and her mother, all wondering the same thing.

Why is Lancelot in chains?

The king cleared his throat. "None of ye are aware of the arrangement I have with Sir Lancelot, thus I see I must explain. After years of loyal fealty, I bequeathed the honor of caring for my sword, the mighty Excalibur, to Sir Lancelot."

The crowd gasped as one, and then held their breath, waiting for their king to continue.

"Oh dear," Leeana exhaled, putting her hand to her mouth. Turning to her mother she asked, "Did father ever tell thee this?"

Leeana's mother shook her head no.

"This has been a closely guarded secret, for I did not want others to know where I kept the holy sword, lest it be stolen. This morning I asked Sir Lancelot to bring me Excalibur…and he returned with only this—" the king held up the jewel-studded scabbard that had been resting on the square table. "Unless someone can prove otherwise, I hereby declare Lancelot a traitor to the Crown and to the Square Table."

Immediately a low rumbling murmur swept across the Judgment Hall as neighbor turned to neighbor to voice their astonishment. Leeana's mother burst into tears.

"That is why Father was in such a state of agitation this morning," Leeana realized. Turning to Ethan and Dallin, she whispered, "When my father departed this morning, he acted as if something was terribly wrong. He instructed me to seek out Merlin, however he failed to expound upon the problem. All he did say was that Merlin would know what to do, and that I should bring him to the Hall of Judgment."

"Merlin?" Ethan interrupted. "Is he coming?"

"Alas, no. I went to the magician's cottage and told him that my father requested his help. But Merlin said he was preoccupied with his cleaning chores, and instructed me to proceed on my journey. When I didst persist, he promised that all would be well. Upon my return home I didst find thee in the armory, delivered by magic in my family's hour of need."

Ethan and Dallin exchanged glances.

"Okay. So, uh, what do you want us to do?" Dallin asked.

"We must go on a journey together, as Merlin counseled, and bring back the king's sword, Excalibur," Leeana said, squeezing Ethan's arm.

"Oh no," Ethan lamented. "Not another adventure."

"Where should we begin to look for Excalibur?" Dallin said enthusiastically.

As if overhearing Dallin's question, a tall blond-haired knight stood and hushed the crowd. "Tell us, Lancelot, where is Excalibur?"

Silence hung in the air as everyone waited for an answer. Even the birds in the rafters stopped chirping, as if they too awaited the outcome of such an important question.

Lancelot bowed his head, the limp brown hair shielding his shame-filled eyes. "I do not know, Sir Tristan."

"How can ye not know when ye were entrusted with the care and protection of the mighty sword?" a red-bearded knight demanded to know, rising from his seat.

Lancelot looked at the man and replied, "Sir Kay, ye know me to be an honest man. If I knew the location of Excalibur, I would not stand before thee in chains."

The knights began talking loudly amongst themselves. Some believed Sir Lancelot to be innocent. Others voiced the opinion that he must be guilty if only he and the king knew where Excalibur was hidden. Still, others argued that Lancelot would not steal the sword and leave the scabbard. Both were together, and both had magical powers. Why steal one piece and return the other?

"What's the big deal about one sword?" Dallin asked. "Your father has lots of swords. Why not give King Arthur one of those?"

Turning her attention away from the square table, she said, "Excalibur is a magic sword."

"If I remember correctly," Ethan said, "Didn't Arthur pull Excalibur out of a stone?"

Leeana shook her head. "No, that was a different sword. As a young lad, Arthur pulled a sword out of a stone. That miraculous event proved he was the true heir of the throne, and king by divine right."

"Yeah, I saw the movie," Dallin said.

Leeana raised an eyebrow, but didn't stop to ask what a movie was. "However, that sword was not Excalibur, and eventually it broke in battle. Thereafter, Merlin sent Arthur on a quest to find the Lady of the Lake. When at last he found her, the Lady searched Arthur's heart, and found him to be a worthy king, and bequeathed to him the mighty Excalibur."

"But now that Arthur is king, why does the sword still matter?" Dallin asked.

"Oh, it matters greatly," said Leeana. "Excalibur is powerful, and whosoever has possession of the sword cannot be defeated in battle. Imagine the consequences if Excalibur were to fall into the wrong hands. No one would be able to stop them."

"So if someone else has Excalibur, King Arthur will not remain king for long," Ethan guessed.

"Ye are correct."

Now the boys understood why the king was so furious over the loss of one sword, and why everyone else was so worried.

A tall, burly knight stood and raised his arms for silence.

"Your Majesty," the knight began. "It mattereth not if Sir Lancelot stole, sold, or lost Excalibur. If the sword hath disappeared, then we art all in danger."

"Hear, hear," many of the other knights said. "Sir Percival is correct," others agreed. Someone from the audience yelled, "All is lost!"

The crowd erupted into a frenzy of shouting and yelling.

"Quiet. QUIET!" Sir Percival bellowed, waving his hands to silence the knights and the unruly crowd. "But perchance Excalibur is only misplaced. If we all go to House Lancelot and search diligently, may we not uncover the sword's whereabouts? Thus all shall not be lost."

"Tear the house down!" a lord sitting next to Dallin yelled, and the crowd erupted into frantic commotion again.

King Arthur stood on the square table and bellowed, "SILENCE!"

There was silence.

"If another spectator maketh one more outburst I shall personally throw that man or woman into the dungeon."

Facing his knights, King Arthur said, "Sir Percival, I grant that ye and five other knights shall go immediately to House Lancelot and search diligently. If Excalibur is found, and hast only been misplaced, I shall grant pardon to Lancelot, and restore him to full fellowship of the square table."

Turning to Lancelot, "But if Excalibur has disappeared, then Lancelot is guilty of treason, and shall suffer the fate of all traitors."

The Hall of Judgment was silent, except for the stifled sobs of Lancelot's wife.

In the silence, a distant trump sounded from the castle walls, followed by horse's hooves galloping across the drawbridge. The horse stopped outside the doors, followed by much shouting and the clanking of armor.

The large doors to the Hall burst open and a disheveled man stumbled in, breathing hard. "Your Highness! Your Highness! I bring news!"

Every head in the Hall of Judgment turned.

Still standing on the square table, King Arthur looked down at the man and commanded, "Speak, herald! What is it?"

Bent over, trying to catch his breath, the messenger gasped, "Excalibur! Your Highness…has been found!"

Lancelot looked up. Leeana's mother cried out in joy. Ethan sighed with relief.

Dallin mumbled, "Rats! So much for another adventure."

Jumping off the table, King Arthur ran to the messenger, pulling him upright. "Where, man? Tell me where!"

Ethan was already making plans to go back home through the traveling trunk when he heard the only three words that could plunge the entire kingdom into immediate chaos.

Holding onto the king's tunic for support, the man cried out in despair, "Morgan le Fay."

CHAPTER 6

Spies

The Hall of Judgment exploded into madness as people abandoned their seats and ran for the doors. When the herald said the name "Morgan le Fay," it was as if he had just unleashed a fire-breathing dragon within the hall. Everyone screamed and ran for their lives.

The Knights of the Square Table grabbed their swords and surrounded the king in a defensive perimeter. King Arthur barked out orders to his soldiers, telling them to secure the castle, send out patrols, bring up the drawbridge, and close the city gates.

Now would have been the perfect opportunity for Sir Lancelot to try and escape, but he just stood there, dumbfounded.

Ethan and Dallin were carried away with the crowd toward the exits.

43

"Ethan! What are we going to do?" Dallin yelled over the commotion.

"I don't know," Ethan shouted back. "But if they close the city gates we will not be able to get back to the traveling trunk. Where is Leeana?"

Dallin pointed to the far side of the room. Leeana was holding her mother's head in her lap, while the handmaid fanned her mistress. Apparently Leeana's mother had fainted.

Fighting their way through the pressing crowd, Ethan and Dallin managed to break free and raced over to Leeana.

"Come on, we have to get back to your house," Ethan urged. He was thinking that now was the perfect time to climb back into the trunk and go home.

"No," Leeana shook her bowed head. "We shall be safest within Camelot. The king shall protect us."

"What about Excalibur?" Dallin asked. He wasn't thinking about returning home, he was thinking about a new adventure. "How can we help your father if we are stuck here in the castle?"

Leeana lifted her tear-stained face and looked into Dallin's excited eyes. Blinking away the tears, she surveyed the situation. Knights were escorting her father back to the dungeon. Her mother had fainted and would be safe here in the castle with her handmaid. She knew Dallin was right. They must find Excalibur. That was the only way to free her father and save Camelot.

Standing with determination, she placed her mother's head gently into the handmaid's arms. "Yes, Dallin doth speak the truth. We must escape before they raise the drawbridge. Follow me."

Grabbing Dallin's hand, who in turn grabbed Ethan's hand, Leeana charged into the crowd of people, bullying her way past everyone.

"She reminds me of Sybullus the Bull," Dallin called over his shoulder.

Ethan laughed. Dallin was right. During their last adventure to Atlantis, Sybullus the Bull had charged through a forest, knocking down trees in his relentless pursuit of the boys. Leeana was doing the same thing now, except she was knocking people out of her way and pulling the boys along with her.

When they finally made it outside the Hall of Judgment, they saw the guards preparing to lift the drawbridge.

"Uh oh, we better hurry or we are going to have to swim the moat," Dallin said, imagining monsters lurking in the murky water.

Sprinting across the courtyard, Ethan's cloak snagged on a thorny rosebush, and he fell, pulling Dallin and Leeana down with him.

The cloak ripped off, leaving Ethan gasping for breath while grasping his throat in pain. Seeing the drawbridge still down, he abandoned his tangled cloak. "Quick, to the gate."

Climbing to their feet, they ran. They didn't get far before someone cried out, "Spies! Mordred spies!"

Ethan no longer had the veil of secrecy his cloak had provided

"Halt!" a soldier barked, running after them. "Seize those squires! Don't let them escape!"

"Faster," Leeana cried. The drawbridge was starting to rise.

Almost there.

A soldier stationed on top of the castle wall released the portcullis, and it dropped with a determined clang over the exit, like the mighty teeth of an iron dragon. Ethan and Dallin jumped onto the gate and started to climb, Leeana right behind. There was a gap large

enough for them to squeeze through at the top, and the drawbridge on the other side was still mostly down. If they could just get over the gate in time they would be free.

"Get down here!" a guard bellowed. He slammed into Leeana, knocking her off the gate, and then yanked Ethan and Dallin down by their ankles. The boys hit the ground hard, the wind knocked out of them.

They were immediately encircled by long spears and sharp swords, all pointing at their necks.

"Please, we are trying to help," Leeana begged, struggling to her feet.

"I can see that," the guard snarled. "Trying to help Morgan le Fay."

"No," Leeana cried out. "We are trying to save my father, and Camelot."

"Take them to the king," he ordered.

The soldiers dragged them back into the Hall of Judgment. It was now empty of spectators. King Arthur and his knights surrounded the square table discussing defensive procedures should Morgan le Fay attack. Leeana's mother remained unconscious on the bench, and Lancelot had already been removed to the dungeon.

"Sire, we found these spies trying to escape," the guard said, pushing Ethan and Dallin forward. One of the other guards held Leeana by the scruff of her neck.

Several knights pulled out their swords, pointing them at the boys.

"Let me just say, you guys are so cool," Dallin said. "Though I really think you should have a round table instead of a square one."

"Silence!" the king ordered. "Do not speak unless ye are spoken to."

He looked at each boy, his scowl finally resting on Leeana. "Ye are Lancelot's daughter, are ye not?"

"Yes, your highness," Leeana said, bowing her head.

"And these are your father's squires?" he accused, pointing to Ethan and Dallin.

"They are my friends," she blurted out. "But they are not what ye think."

"Do not tell me what to think!" the king commanded. "This further proves that thy father is a traitor. Did Lancelot tell thee to sneak Mordred's squires into my castle to spy on me? Or are ye taking orders directly from Morgan le Fay?"

"No, your Majesty. My friends are not here to spy on thee," Leeana said. "Call upon thy magician and ask him thyself. Merlin sent them to help save Excalibur."

"Lies, lies, lies!" the king raged. "Throw them into the dungeon."

"Nooo!" Leeana screamed as they were dragged away.

CHAPTER 7

The Dungeon

The dungeon laid buried deep beneath the castle. The stale, musty air smelled like an old trash can that had never been emptied.

Before being abandoned in their cold cell, Ethan, Dallin and Leeana had their feet shackled to the dingy floor. They could stand, but the sloped roof made it uncomfortable, and the chains weren't long enough to afford them much movement. A dying torch flickered outside their cell, providing just enough light for the prisoners to see how bad their predicament was.

"Why does the traveling trunk keep dumping us in places that are falling apart?" Ethan wondered out loud. "You know, this is the second time in a week we've been thrown into a prison."

"I know," Dallin said excitedly. He removed his backpack from underneath the cloak and rummaged through it. Fortunately their guards hadn't searched them. "Isn't it cool?"

"No, it is *not* cool," Ethan said grumpily. He used his thumb and middle finger to flick away a cockroach that was crawling up his leg.

"Thy brother is correct," Leeana said to Ethan. "It is very cold down here."

"No, that is not what Dallin means," Ethan said. "He thinks the dungeon is cool, as in neat. When we say 'cool' what we really mean is neat."

"Oh," she said. "Well, then Dallin is not correct."

"I couldn't agree with you more."

"No," Leeana asserted. "The dungeon is not neat at all. Indeed, it is very filthy and unclean. I dare say it has not been swept or mopped since it was first built."

Dallin laughed at Leeana's misunderstanding, and then added, "Yeah, if Mom were here, she would whip King Arthur into shape and make him clean up this dungeon before dinner."

"No, Leeana, that is not what I mean by neat," Ethan said, ignoring his brother's comment. "When we say 'neat' what we really mean is awesome. Dallin thinks the dungeon is awesome."

The poor girl was really confused now. "I do not understand 'ahh-sum.'"

"Awesome," Ethan repeated. "You know, it means cool, neat, amazing, wonderful, all those things put together into one word."

"Ye are making my head hurt," Leeana said. "Why do ye not just say what ye mean to say the first time instead of using many words that have different meanings?"

"Forget it," Ethan said. "My head is starting to hurt too."

"Well then, how about we get out of here?" Dallin said standing in front of Ethan, free of his chains.

"Hey, how did you escape?"

"My backpack," Dallin said. "Remember, we packed the emergency kit before we left."

"You're right!" Ethan said. "But I never saw you pack a metal cutting saw."

"I didn't. But I did bring sunblock," he said, holding up a pink bottle.

"Sunblock? How is sunblock going to help us? We're imprisoned in a dungeon."

"Astounding! Can ye truly block the sun?" Leeana asked, wonder in her voice. "Ye must be more powerful than even Merlin."

Ignoring Leeana's comment, Dallin said, "Take your boot off, rub the sunblock on your leg, and you should be able to slide right out of the chains. The lotion makes everything slippery."

"Dallin, you're brilliant," Ethan said, removing his boot. "What else did you bring?"

Squirting sunblock onto Ethan's leg, Dallin said, "I brought some rope, our old firecrackers, the whale vomit from Atlantis—here take a whiff, it makes this place smell a lot better—a lighter, some duct tape, scissors, one of your notebooks, and a flashlight."

He turned on the flashlight.

"Oh, I can see," Leeana said, shielding her eyes from the bright light. "Ye truly are magicians."

Ethan jumped up and put his boot back on. "Now how are we going to open the door?"

Dallin helped free Leeana from her chains, and then held out his suggestion for obtaining their freedom. "How about a firecracker?"

"Let's give it a try," Ethan said. Brushing flakes of rust off the prison door keyhole, he stuffed in the firecracker.

"Get to the back of the cell, close your eyes and cover your ears," Ethan said. He lit the fuse and ran.

KA-BOOM!

The metal door lurched and then slowly creaked open.

"Wow, that was loud," Dallin said. "We better hurry; the guards probably heard that."

Sure enough, orders to search the dungeon drifted down the winding stairs. The other prisoners, startled by the unusual explosion, began rattling their prison doors, adding confusion to the commotion.

"Quick, go deeper into the dungeon," Ethan said, pushing everyone down the corridor.

Dallin led, his flashlight lighting the way as they ran around a corner and down another flight of stairs.

"Do dungeons ever have back doors?" Ethan asked.

"I do not know," Leeana puffed. "This is the first dungeon I have ever been in."

Reaching a dead end, they stopped and listened. They could not hear anyone coming. The guards must have stopped to investigate their empty cell.

"Maybe we can hide in one of these cells down here for awhile, and then sneak out when things calm down," Dallin suggested.

"Good idea," Leeana said, heading for the closest prison door.

"Mmhhhggg," Leeana shrieked in terror as a hand shot through the bars and clamped tightly over her mouth.

"Hush!" a voice whispered urgently.

Dallin shone his beam on the face pressed tightly to the prison bars. The man blinked at the bright light, turning his head away.

"Lancelot!" Ethan said.

The man released his daughter.

"Oh, father!" Leeana cried, reaching through the bars to hug him.

"No time for pleasantries," he said, pulling back from Leeana so that he could get a better look at her and her companions. "Why are ye here?"

"King Arthur believes my friends are spies for Mordred, but really they were sent by Merlin," Leeana said, pointing to Ethan and Dallin.

"Ye are not spies?" he asked, eyeing the coat of arms on their tunics.

"No, sir," Ethan said. "How can we help you escape?"

"I cannot escape. If I leave, it shall prove my guilt. I must remain, but ye three can prove me innocent."

"How Father?" Leeana asked.

"Excalibur," he said. "Ye must find Excalibur. That is the only way to prove my innocence and save Camelot."

"But Father, how do we escape from the dungeon?"

"I helped Arthur build this castle. There are secret passageways throughout, even here in the dungeon." Sticking his arm through the prison bars, he pointed at the dead end. "That wall hast a metal ring mounted to the lowest right stone."

Dallin panned the wall with his flashlight, catching a glint of metal.

"We see the ring," Ethan announced.

"Pull that stone out and ye shall find a tunnel. It shall lead thee to the outer walls of the castle."

Leeana held the light while Ethan and Dallin grabbed the ring and gave it a good yank.

"It's not budging," Dallin grunted.

Voices began to draw nearer. The guards were starting to search the lower parts of the dungeon.

"Ye can do it! Pull harder!" Lancelot whispered encouragingly. "Leeana, help them."

Handing the flashlight to Lancelot, Leeana joined the boys. Placing their feet against the wall as leverage, they pulled as hard as they could. The stone slowly slid out. There was another metal ring mounted on the inside of the stone to pull it back into place

"Quickly, ye must flee at once!" Lancelot said, frantically waving them away.

Ethan and Leeana crawled through the hole. Dallin grabbed his flashlight and ran, but was forced to stop abruptly when Lancelot did not let go. Their eyes locked. The knight's brown eyes bored into Dallin's green ones.

Footsteps began echoing down the stone stairwell.

"I am counting on thee. Whether they know it or not, all of Camelot is counting on thee." He released the flashlight.

Dallin nodded to Lancelot, and then dove into the tunnel after his companions.

As they pulled the stone back into place, they heard Lancelot whisper, "Take care of my daughter, brave squires."

CHAPTER 8

Escape from Camelot

Pushing out a thin stone that concealed the secret exit, Ethan crawled onto a ledge. After his eyes adjusted to the bright sunlight, he reached back into the tunnel and pulled Leeana and Dallin out. Their knees were sore and their backs ached from the long crawl.

The secret passageway released them at the back of the castle where no guards had been posted.

"Uh oh," Dallin said.

"What's wrong?" asked Ethan.

Dallin pointed. "The moat. We still have to cross the moat."

"That's no big deal. You know how to swim."

"But what about moat monsters? I think I saw something swimming in the moat when we crossed earlier today."

"There is no such thing as moat monsters. You probably just saw a tree branch floating in the water," Ethan said.

Leeana looked worried too.

"Look, I'll swim across first, and then you two follow. Okay?" Ethan said. He removed his boots and tossed them across the moat. "See you on the other side."

Diving off the ledge into the murky water, he breast-stroked to the shore.

Dallin watched for any unusual disturbances in the water. There were none.

"What did I tell you?" Ethan called out. "Completely safe."

Dallin looked at Leeana. "Do you want to go together, or one at a time?"

"Uh, I am not sure if I can do this," she said nervously.

Stuffing his cloak into his backpack, Dallin said, "You'll be fine, there's no moat monster. I must have seen a log, like Ethan said."

"No, it is not that..."

"Here, catch Ethan," Dallin said, throwing his bag across the moat. "Then what's the problem?"

"I cannot swim."

"Oh. Uh, Ethan," Dallin called out, "Leeana can't swim."

Ethan thought for a minute. "Can you float?"

"Ye-yes, I believe so."

Ethan removed the rope from Dallin's backpack and threw it back to him. "Tie the rope around her waist and throw me the end. I'll pull her across."

"Are you okay with that, Leeana?" Dallin asked.

"Yes, I trust that ye and Ethan shall protect me."

Dallin tied a bowline knot around Leeana's waist. He had learned in Cub Scouts that this knot would not slip or jam, perfect for pulling someone across a moat. He smiled, knowing that his Den Leader would be proud.

Holding the rope, he lowered Leeana into the moat.

"Take a deep breath and try to keep your head above the water," Dallin suggested. He threw the other end of the rope to Ethan. "Okay! Pull away."

Three minutes later Leeana crawled out of the moat, coughing and a little waterlogged. Her head had gone under a few times, but she had managed not to panic.

Dallin scanned the moat one last time, and then jumped in feet first. He sank like a rock into the murky water. His feet hit the bottom of the moat and sank another foot into the squishy muck. He kicked off and bolted for the surface. Despite Ethan's reassurances, Dallin still felt nervous. Breathing rapidly, he swam as quickly as he could, until his arm brushed against something firm but slimy.

"Ahh," he yelled, stopping in the middle of the moat.

"Dallin, come on," Ethan encouraged.

"There's something swimming around me."

"It's just your imagination. Come on!" Ethan said. "Here, I'll throw you the rope."

"O-okay," Dallin said, his teeth chattering, and not just because of the cold water.

Ethan threw the rope, the end landing in front of Dallin. He reached for it, and as he did so, the rope began to rise from the water.

"AAAHH!" Dallin screamed. "Moat monster!"

A giant scaly head connected to a long eel-like body rose from the murky water.

"Kheeeee," it hissed, forked tongue flicking between saber-toothed fangs. Tasting Dallin's scent, the beast stared at him with its massive black eyes.

"Hey! Hey! Over here!" Ethan yelled, waving his arms at the moat monster. He reached into Dallin's backpack, grabbed the first thing he could find and threw it. Dallin's flashlight wacked the monster on the side of the head and plunked into the water. The beast swung its head toward Ethan, hissed and then dove back into the murky depths.

"Swim, Dallin! Swim!" Leeana yelled.

Dallin paddled like a champion swim dog, getting closer to the shore; but the moat monster wasn't done. It swam underneath Dallin lifting his entire body out of the water, and then flipped him back into the middle of the moat with its tail. Dallin sank beneath the surface.

"Do something!" Leeana shouted to Ethan.

With a firecracker in one hand, and the lighter in the other, Ethan ran into the moat. Dallin resurfaced and began swimming.

"Hurry, Dallin!" Ethan yelled.

The moat monster swam underneath Dallin and lifted him up in the air again, but this time Dallin wrapped his arms around its thick neck and held on, squeezing tight.

"Hold on, Dallin!" Leeana screamed.

The monster dove into the water with Dallin on its back. The moat became still as death.

Thirty seconds passed. Then one minute.

"Where did they go?" Ethan said frantically.

Like an exploding depth charge, the moat monster burst from the water, Dallin clinging to its back. He rode the beast like a cowboy on a bucking bronco.

Instead of diving again, the monster rose higher out of the water and swung its head from side to side, trying to throw Dallin off.

"HELP!" Dallin screamed, starting to slide down the slimy skin. He grabbed part of the monster's dorsal fin and hung on.

"Kheeeee," it hissed again. Opening its mouth wide it snapped at Dallin, trying to bite his leg.

Ethan saw his opportunity. He lit the firecracker and threw it at the beast. It sailed between the long fangs, landing in the monster's mouth. The beast swallowed, reared back, and lunged at Dallin. Its razor sharp fangs caught the edge of his boot, and yanked him off its back.

Dallin plummeted blindly into the brackish water, kicking and swinging his arms. He gasped for air as

his head surfaced and began backstroking away from the monster. The beast looked down at its escaping prey, opened its mouth, and attacked.

Dallin's scream was silenced by a muffled ka-boom as the firecracker exploded in the belly of the beast. Smoke gushed from the monster's nostrils, and it collapsed into the moat, sending small waves of water to the shore.

Ethan dove into the moat and dragged Dallin out.

Collapsing in the muddy cattails, Dallin coughed up water, trying to find enough oxygen to speak. "Remind me...remind me to never swim in moats again."

CHAPTER 9
Valley of Wailing Mists

Sneaking around the castle, they found their horses where they had stabled them, and quickly rode away. Soldiers were marching out of the city to patrol the borders of Camelot. This left the city gates open long enough for them to escape.

They made a quick stop at House Lancelot where Leeana changed out of her soggy court clothes. Afraid of being recognized out in the open, she exchanged dresses with one of her maids.

Galloping along a winding road through the forest, Ethan finally asked, "So what's the plan?"

"We shall sneak into Morgan's stronghold, Castle deOrk in the Valley of Wailing Mists, find Excalibur, return it to King Arthur and save my father," Leeana said without skipping a beat.

"What?" Ethan said. "Are you joking?"

Looking at Ethan with a confused look on her face, she said, "I did not tell a joke. Why dost thou think I am joking?"

"How are we going to break into a castle? They've got moats, and guards, and drawbridges and everything," Ethan said. "We almost died trying to break *out* of a castle, I'm sure it is going to be much harder breaking into one."

"I am *not* swimming in any more moats," Dallin said.

"We cannot break into the castle, it is made of stone. That would be too difficult, even with thy magic," Leeana said, not understanding Ethan's use of the phrase "break into."

It was Dallin's turn to explain. "What Ethan means is how are we going to *sneak* into the castle?"

"Oh. Why did ye not say so? That shall be easy. Both of ye are wearing Mordred's coat of arms. Ye should be able to walk right into Castle deOrk without any problem."

"Oh yeah, I forgot about the clothes," Ethan admitted. "But what about the Valley of Wailing Mists? What's that all about?"

Leeana looked at the boys in astonishment. "Ye really do not know about the mists?"

"No," they answered.

"And who's Morgan le Fay? I've never heard of her," Dallin said.

"If I remember correctly, she is the oldest step-sister of King Arthur," Ethan said.

"True," Leeana confirmed. "When Arthur pulled the sword from the stone, he was chosen to be king. Morgan was not happy about her younger step-brother obtaining the thrown, for she felt the kingdom belonged to her. But she was already married to Lord Uriens, who hailed from the land of Gore. His home, Castle Tauroc, was far from Camelot.

"Morgan was unhappy in Gore, and desired to return to Camelot. After several years, she convinced her husband that he should be king of Camelot, and herself queen. Moreover, as the eldest sibling, she felt she deserved the throne. Deceived by Morgan's cunning, her husband raised an army and attacked Camelot. King Arthur defeated him, with the help of Excalibur, and banished Morgan from the land forever."

"So how come she is back?" Dallin asked.

"Morgan was gone for many years. Then one day a damsel arrived at the castle with a marvelous mantle bejeweled with precious stones. She offered it as a gift for Lady Guinevere, a token of friendship from Morgan le Fay, and a sign of her repentant heart."

"What's a mantle?" asked Dallin.

"It's like a scarf," Ethan said.

"King Arthur was pleased to offer forgiveness to his step-sister, and accepted the mantle. He was about to place it around his wife's shoulders when my father intervened. He demanded that Morgan's damsel wear it first. As soon as it touched her shoulders, she instantly turned to stone."

"Wasn't there a statue in the castle courtyard wearing a jeweled scarf?" asked Ethan.

"The very same. King Arthur placed the stone damsel in the courtyard to serve as a reminder of Morgan's treachery."

"You still haven't told us about the Valley of Wailing Mists," Dallin said.

"Patience, Dallin. I was about to tell of that."

Leeana took a minute to get her bearings, and then led the group off the road and onto a game trail that diverged into the thick forest.

73

"After the incident with the mantle, King Arthur sent the Knights of the Square Table on a valiant quest to seek out Morgan and bring her to justice. A year later, only half of them returned, all empty-handed.

"They reported that Morgan did take refuge in the Valley of Wailing Mists at the base of Helscynth Mountain. It is an accursed place, from which floweth a foul waterfall. The brackish water is so putrid that nothing doth live or swim in its depths. Nor do any plants grow from its banks, and the earth itself refuses to drink it up."

"Sound's like Ethan's bath water," Dallin chuckled.

"Quit joking. This is serious stuff," Ethan said, hanging on Leeana's every word.

Leeana continued, "Legend doeth speak of demons born in the mists that billow from the base of the waterfall. Purportedly, they have been tamed by Morgan, and sent to feast upon the memories of mortals. Some believe that the knights who did not return to Camelot wander in the mists to this very day, wailing because they have forgotten who they are."

"Wicked," Dallin shuddered, a chill creeping up his spine.

"Morgan's new home," Leeana said, "is Castle deOrk, also known as the Fortress of Darkness. It is believed to be made from the black stone of Helscynth Mountain, and the mists are the only guards needed to protect it from invasion."

"Whoa," Ethan said, reining in his horse. He was having serious second thoughts about helping Leeana. "This is crazy. You actually think three kids can sneak into Morgan's castle and get Excalibur back, when even King Arthur's knights have failed?"

"Of course," Leeana answered, looking over her shoulder, but not stopping. "That is why Merlin sent thee here as Mordred's squires."

Facing forward, she continued deeper into the forest.

Ethan sat on his horse pondering Leeana's words.

Could this all be true? He thought to himself. Questions swirled in his mind as he tried to figure out what he knew from the legends of King Arthur, and what Leeana was telling him.

Merlin didn't send us here. The traveling trunk did. Then another thought struck him. *Is the traveling trunk sending us on these adventures so we can change history, thereby changing the future, or are we here by some random chance? If Dallin and I hadn't come back, would the stories be different?*

If we turned around right now and went home would the legends of King Arthur still exist, or would they be about Morgan le Fay instead?

As more thoughts spilled into Ethan's mind, his head began to swim. *If Morgan conquers Camelot, will that change my future? Or does history already know that Dallin and I would come, and we are now here in Camelot to make sure that history happens as we already know it? If that is the case, then we cannot fail since in our future Morgan does not win. King Arthur and the Knights of the Round Table are what my future holds. I should have nothing to worry about. I hope.*

Bolstered by these thoughts, Ethan looked up to see Dallin and Leeana disappearing through a thick tangle of branches.

"Hey, wait for me!" he yelled, spurring his horse forward. *If we come out of this alive, somehow I'll have to get King Arthur to change the square table into a round one.*

Catching up, he overheard Dallin talking. "Evil sorceress, ruthless knights, mist demons; this would be the coolest adventure ever if we ran into a dragon."

Leeana laughed. "Thou art a funny boy, Dallin. There are no such things as dragons."

Ethan sighed with relief.

CHAPTER 10

Castle de Orc

The lush forest gradually faded, the trees growing yellow and sickly-looking the closer they got to the jagged peaks of Helscynth Mountain. The air became heavy, and the horses' breathing labored as thick mists swirled across their path. Like a bad dream, the forest eventually morphed into a graveyard of skeletal trees that were withered and leafless.

The three companions urged their horses onward through the dismal wasteland. Despite the risk of being seen, they chose to ride along the hilltops, avoiding the lowlands which boiled with the eerie mists.

A mile from the castle, an oasis of healthy oak trees sprung from the barren ground, defying their dismal surroundings, refusing to wither and die like everything else. The thick grove of trees guarded a small spring of fresh water, as if protecting it from invasion. Seeking refuge, the horses plodded into the cluster of oaks and refused to go any further.

As the horses drank from the spring, Dallin slid off his mount and moaned, "Ow. I don't think I am going to be able to sit for a week."

"I didn't know horseback riding was so painful," Ethan said, wobbling bowlegged to a tree. He leaned against it and massaged his hamstrings.

After the horses were refreshed, Leeana tied them to a thick branch. "Stretch thy legs and ye shall quickly regain thy strength."

Through the clump of trees they could see a towering black castle shrouded in swirling mists.

"So, that is Castle deOrk," Ethan said, goose bumps running up his arms. "It doesn't look very friendly."

Instead of a large sprawling city like Camelot, Morgan's dilapidated castle was a mass of splintered towers protruding from the black cliffs of the mountain like jagged teeth. A filthy river cascaded down the serrated cliffs, crashing upon sharp rocks where mountain and castle merged. Clouds of mist billowed from the waterfall, swirling around the

castle, giving it a haunted look. Though it was still early afternoon, and the sun blazed in the misty sky above, Castle deOrk was shrouded in an eerie shadow, making everything look distorted.

"The gate is open, but I do not see any guards," Leeana said. "The ramparts are deserted."

"What about the mists?" Ethan said nervously.

"I don't hear any wailing; maybe they only attack at night. Besides, thou wearest Mordred's coat of arms. If the mists serve Morgan le Fay, we should be able to get through them without any problem."

"Come on then. Let's go," Dallin said, leading the way out of the trees.

Crossing an open field, they made a beeline for the castle gates. Running helped relieve the riding cramps in their legs.

As they got closer, they could see that the mountain river circled the castle, creating a natural moat, before resuming its journey into the valley. Fortunately, the drawbridge was down and unguarded, except for the thick mists that prowled the ground.

As they walked through the poorly lit gateway, Ethan said, "Wow, this is going to be easier than I thought."

Passing into the inner courtyard, the shadows and mists disappeared, replaced by a wave of heat and noise. The small castle they had seen from the forest unveiled itself to be a towering fortress cut deep into the cliffs of the mountain. Giant fire pits littered a vast courtyard inside the castle walls, from which metal was being smelted and prepared by hundreds of workers. The bang and clang of swords and armor being crafted filled the air. In every direction they looked, craftsmen and soldiers toiled over their labors.

Morgan le Fay was preparing for war.

"Wow," Dallin exclaimed. "Now that is what I call magic. Morgan sure fooled us."

"Curses! I should have known she would place a spell over her castle," Leeana said. "Come. We must retreat and make a new plan."

Turning around, Ethan crashed into a towering man in black armor.

"What are ye doing here?" the knight demanded. His voice boomed from a large black helmet that resembled an upside down witch's cauldron with a few horizontal slits cut into it. "It was my understanding that Sir Mordred had taken all of his squires to conscript more soldiers from amongst the peasants."

Ethan and Dallin stared at the giant in stunned silence. There wasn't much to see since he was covered in black armor from head to toe. Even his thick hands were encased with black metal gauntlets.

Leeana prodded Ethan in the back.

"Uh, we are Sir Mordred's squires," Ethan blurted out.

"I knoweth that," the Black Knight said. "I beheld Mordred's coat of arms on your tunics. Do ye think me a buffoon?"

"Nuh-no sir," Ethan mumbled.

"Then enlighten me. Why have ye returned? Is Sir Mordred having trouble?"

"Ye-yes," Ethan stuttered, not sure what else to say. "Yes, Sir Mordred is having trouble."

The Black Knight made a strange whirring noise, and then smashed his giant metal fist into his opposite open palm. The loud, sudden movement caused Ethan and Dallin to jump. "The Queen thought he might meet resistance from the peasants. Come with me."

Ethan and Dallin exchanged glances. There was nothing to do except follow the imposing black knight. He led them through a maze of workers and soldiers toward the razor-sharp cliffs that loomed at the back of the castle courtyard.

"Who is this guy?" Dallin whispered over the clanking sound of the knight's armor.

"The Black Knight is Accolon, Morgan's personal body guard," Leeana whispered as they entered a tunnel carved into the dark stone. "I thought he was just a rumor. No one has ever seen him before, or at least no one has seen him and survived."

Ethan gulped. "Is he taking us to the dungeon?"

"I do not believe so. If he thought we were spies we would already be dead," Leeana whispered. "But keep thine eyes open for an escape."

The tunnel yawned, becoming a massive hall carved from the mountain. Torches sputtered along the rough-hewn walls, fighting desperately to keep the dancing shadows at bay. The chamber was similar to the Hall of Judgment in size and layout, but that is where the similarities ended.

There were no windows. In the center of the hall sat a large rectangular table bowing before a raised black throne inlaid with twisted silver carvings. Along the walls were long tapestries depicting epic battles between men and foul beasts. Ogres and goblins pillaged towns, giants squashed knights in shining armor, and dragons rained fire from the sky. The monsters were victorious, led by a black-haired witch wielding a glowing blue sword.

Pulling a torch from its mount, Accolon marched to the back of the hall where a winding stairwell spiraled upward into the mountain. Turning to the boys, he noticed Leeana for the first time. "What are ye doing here, girl? All maids must report to the kitchen. There is much cooking to be done for the queen's armies!"

Grabbing Ethan and Dallin by the scruff of their necks, he pushed them forward and herded them up the stairs. Leeana watched in despair as they disappeared up the twisting tunnel. Turning around, she ran out of the gloomy hall.

CHAPTER 11

Morgan le Fay

Up and up Ethan and Dallin climbed. Every time they began to slow down the Black Knight would make a whirring sound and slam a fist into an open palm. He seemed to really enjoy hitting things.

What are we going to do without Leeana? Ethan thought, trying to come up with a plan.

Dallin wondered the same thing, but since he couldn't think of a solution, he started counting steps. He stopped after he reached two hundred, a new distraction consuming his attention: his legs muscles were burning. Stealing a glace at Ethan, he knew his brother felt the same way. After the long horseback ride, these stairs were a further challenge to their already sore legs.

Accolon finally pushed them off the stairs and onto a level of tunnels that branched into several hallways. Toward the end of the central hallway two soldiers stood at attention outside a set of massive iron doors.

Approaching the guards with Ethan and Dallin in tow, Accolon demanded, "Announce my arrival to the queen."

The guards looked at each other nervously, their faces paling.

"Bu-but the queen sleepeth," one of them stammered.

"Do ye think me a buffoon?" Accolon asked, the whirring sound starting again as he clenched a fist. "I know she sleepeth. Dost thou think I would march all the way up those stairs if I did not bring her urgent tidings?"

The guards quivered in their armor.

"Wake her, now!" he exploded, punching one of the soldiers with his huge gauntleted fist. The front of the guard's metal breastplate caved in as he went flying down the hall. He landed in a crumpled heap on the stone floor.

Accolon thrust his torch at the remaining guard.

The guard gulped and took the torch. Hands trembling, he turned the handle.

As the iron doors creaked open, a wave of icy air whooshed from the room, sending goose bumps up the boy's arms and a shiver down their spines. Accompanying the surge of cold air was the foul odor of raw sewage. The guard's pale face turned green as he entered the black abyss. Pushing the children into the room behind the guard, Accolon did not seem bothered in the least by the stench or the cold.

The faint firelight from the guard's torch revealed an expansive room. Most of it remained hidden in shadows until the guard threw open the thick curtains. Misty sunlight filtered in, momentarily blinding Ethan and Dallin. Blinking rapidly as his eyes adjusted, Ethan surveyed the room, his gaze resting on a beautiful woman sleeping peacefully upon a four-poster bed. A thick eye-mask shielded her eyes.

Morgan le Fay had wild black hair that shimmered in the sunlight, skin like milk, and an angelic face. She wore a red sequined dress that reflected like millions of tiny rubies. In a word, she was exquisite.

Until she awoke.

She stretched her dainty arms and took a deep, raspy breath. She paused, sniffed the air several times, and then spoke.

"Who dares interrupt my beauty sleep?"

Ethan and Dallin cringed, wanting to cover their ears. The very sound of her voice made them wince with pain. The woman was a rare beauty, but she radiated feelings of dread and hopelessness like a salt-covered slug oozes slime.

"Mu-my Queen," the guard mumbled, bowing to the floor.

"My Queen," Accolon said, cutting off the soldier and waving him away. He fled for the doors, closing them with a hollow boom on his way out. "Sir Mordred is having trouble with your peasants."

"Then ye tell Sir Mordred to give my peasants some trouble," Morgan rasped, her voice making the boys feel like they needed to clear their own throats.

Rising off the bed, she removed the eye-mask. The boys gasped. Her face was beautiful, there was no doubt about that, but her gaze was disturbing. Her left eye was a radiant blue, perfectly normal. But her right eye had withered and sunk deep into its socket, glowing with a sickly yellow light from inside her skull.

"These squires bring a message," Accolon said mechanically, pushing Ethan and Dallin forward.

Morgan considered them with a frown, rapping her fingers on the bed-side table. Her yellow eye pulsed and bulged in its socket as she focused on each boy in turn. She seemed to be looking straight through them. "What doth Mordred require?"

Ethan squirmed under the scrutiny of her unnerving glare. His head began to throb as if something was trying to knock its way in. Then ideas began to take shape in his mind, and he was about to tell Morgan the truth about who they really were, when Dallin broke the spell.

"Excalibur…" Dallin blurted out, taking deep breaths. "Sir Mordred needs Excalibur."

Morgan stared at the boys for a minute longer before turning to a platter of fruit on the table. Her nails, long and filed to sharp points, speared an apple. She sniffed the fruit apprehensively, then took a bite with razor-sharp teeth. The crunch of the apple sounded like bones breaking.

"Why doth he require Excalibur?"

Dallin wasn't sure how to answer. There had never been a plan should they get caught.

"Be-because the peasants are afraid," Ethan said, his brain finally kicking in. Now that he could think clearly a plan began to take shape. "If Mordred has Excalibur with him, the peasants will see who possesses the real power. Then they will have no choice but to join your forces."

"This is foolishness," Morgan said, stabbing several grapes, one after another until she had three of them on one long nail. "Mordred knows the sword is a fake, and if that buffoon of a king, Arthur, finds his real sword, then my entire scheme shall be ruined."

A quick look passed between the boys.

"But the peasants don't know that," Dallin said.

"Right. If you give us Excalibur, we will take it to Sir Mordred, who will then use the fake sword to make the people think he has the real one, and then you will have the soldiers you need to defeat Arthur," Ethan rambled as quickly as he could.

Grabbing a small melon and stalking over to the boys, Morgan le Fay said, "I do not want to defeat Arthur—I wish to crush him. I long for the day when I shall destroy his pretty little kingdom and enslave his people. And if all goes according to plan, tomorrow I shall obliterate Camelot and all the good people in it!"

She crushed the melon in her hand, juice and seeds squirting out from between her fingers and onto the boys' tunics.

Ethan and Dallin gulped nervously.

Leaning forward, her sinister eye burning bright yellow, she flashed a beautiful, treacherous smile. "It is refreshing to see young squires who wish to help me fulfill my dreams. But before I give thee Excalibur, tell me this. Why did Mordred send squires to do a knight's job, especially two squires whom I have never seen before?"

Despite the frigid air in the room, Ethan began to sweat. "I do not know…it is not my position to question my master."

Morgan considered his response. Turning to Accolon she asked, "Do ye have some dispensable squires about?"

"Yes," Accolon responded automatically, obediently awaiting further orders.

Running her fingernail along Ethan's cheek, a vicious smile curled the edges of her lips. "Sir Mordred employs the most talented squires. If these two speak the truth, then they shall have no problem defeating two of thy squires. Go! Prepare the tournament field. I am in the mood for some games."

CHAPTER 12

Cheesy Plans

"This is so cool," Dallin said, selecting a bow that wasn't too big for him. "We get to compete in a medieval tournament!"

The boys were in a tent outside the castle walls, preparing for the contest of their lives. Soldiers roamed the grounds in packs thicker than fleas on a stray cat; otherwise Ethan would have already tried to run away.

Not that he could have run away even if there weren't any soldiers. He was dressed in chain mail and heavy metal armor, making it almost impossible to walk. "I would rather be at home reading about a medieval tournament than actually have to compete in one."

Dallin still wore his squire clothes, with the cloak concealing his backpack.

"Come on Ethan, we could never do this at home," Dallin said, tugging on a bow string. "If Mom knew we were about to fight with swords and arrows we would be grounded for a month."

"Exactly! If we were grounded at least we wouldn't have to fight."

The rules were simple. They would compete in two events: jousting and archery. Dallin and one of Accolon's squire were to shoot at a target 100 paces away. The one with the most arrows closest to the bull's eye would win.

Ethan would joust. He and a second squire would attempt to knock each other off their horses using long blunt sticks called lances. If Dallin and Ethan beat the squires, they would be given the fake Excalibur, and escorted back to Mordred. If they lost, they would suffer for eternity in the clutches of the Wailing Mists.

"We need to find a way to escape," Ethan said. "I've only read about medieval tournaments. I don't know how to compete in one, let alone win."

"But Ethan, if we run away, who is going to save Camelot?" Dallin asked.

"And who is going to save my father?"

Spinning around, Leeana walked through the tent flaps carrying a platter of food and a water bag.

Dallin rushed the girl. "Food! Great, I'm starving."

"I can only stay for a brief moment. It shall arouse suspicion if I am in here too long," Leeana said. Dallin took the platter and dug into the pile of bread and cheese.

"I'm glad you found us," Ethan said. "What are we going to do?"

"My apologies for getting thee into this misfortune," she said, genuine concern on her face. "However I am confident ye shall defeat Sir Accolon's squires, reclaim Excalibur, and then save the kingdom and my father."

"Humph. Not likely," Ethan said. "I can barely stay on a horse. How am I supposed to knock someone else off theirs? Besides, Excalibur is a fake. This whole tournament is pointless!"

"Now it is ye who art joking," Leeana said, "Though I do not find thy joke funny in the least."

"No, really," Dallin mumbled, his mouth full of cheese. "Morgan told us herself that the sword she has is a fake, and if Arthur ever finds his real sword, her plan will fail."

"What?" Leeana asked, confused.

Ethan finished connecting the dots for her. "That is why she is preparing so quickly for war. She has to strike while everyone still thinks she has Excalibur. She is using a fake sword to rally more soldiers, and plans on attacking Camelot tomorrow."

Leeana sat down, pondering the turn of events. Suddenly she leapt to her feet. "This is wonderful news. It meaneth that my father is innocent! But alas, where is the real sword?"

"Who cares about Excalibur," Ethan said. "We still have to figure out a way to get out of here alive."

Leeana's excitement faded. "Ye are right. But what shall we do? All of Castle deOrk's citizens have gathered for the tournament. Escape would be impossible."

"I have an idea," Dallin said, removing his backpack from underneath his cloak. "But you gotta try this cheese first—it's delicious. It has little holes in it, like Swiss cheese."

Ethan took a bite. "Mmm, kind of crunchy."

"Oh, I did hope ye would enjoy this cheese. I found it hidden away in Morgan's kitchen. It is fermented goat's head milk, curdled and aged to perfection after

several years. Fly larvae doth create all the holes, thereby allowing the cheese to rot from the inside. It is quite a delicacy."

"Blahhh," both boys gagged, spitting everywhere.

"Yuck," Ethan said, wiping his tongue on his metal-plated arm. "Dallin, I hope your plan is better than this cheese."

CHAPTER 13

The Tournament

The tournament field was a long, level strip of dead weeds that stretched from the river to the forest. The mists had retreated off the field, as if commanded to do so. They swirled along the boundaries, anxious to regain their lost territory.

The only time peasants got a break from their work was at tournament time, so the event was naturally well attended. Everyone was there.

Trumpets sounded as Ethan and Dallin were escorted out of the tent and onto the field. With his faceplate up, Ethan trotted out on a dapple-brown horse. He carried a long lance pointed skyward. Dallin walked beside him carrying a bow and quiver full of arrows. The awaiting crowd erupted into loud applause as they celebrated the opening of the tournament.

Dallin lifted his hands and waved to the audience. It seemed like everyone was set to have a good time; everyone except Ethan.

The boys stopped in front of a raised platform whereon sat Morgan le Fay, Sir Accolon, and several knights who would act as tournament judges should there be a dispute. The escorting soldier bowed to the platform and then retreated off the field. Dallin bowed, then waved to the crowd again. The audience cheered their approval. Accolon's squires had yet to come out of their tent.

"Don't get so excited, Dallin. What if we don't win?" Ethan said through clenched teeth.

"Of course we are going to win. My plan is perfect." Dallin said. "Leeana will sabotage the squire's arrows so they don't fly straight, that way I win the shooting contest. Then she will pour sunblock on the other squire's lance so he can't hold on to it. That way you won't have to worry about him knocking you off your horse, and can concentrate on winning the joust."

Ethan was not convinced. Dallin's plan had more holes in it than the rotten cheese. He hoped that the delay of Accolon's squires did not mean that Leeana had been caught.

"I sure hope that girl pulls it off, or we are all goners," Ethan whispered.

The crowd began to cheer again. A tall squire walked across the field, but he was coming from the direction of the castle. In his hand he held a long bow, with a quiver of arrows strapped to his back. Joining the boys in front of the platform, he bowed to his queen.

Uh oh, the squire didn't come from the tent. Maybe Leeana was not able to sabotage his arrows, Dallin thought. He exchanged a troubled look with Ethan.

His thoughts were interrupted by more cheering. Accolon's tent flap opened and an armored squire rode out on a large stallion. He did not appear to be having any difficulties with his lance.

Ethan groaned.

The mounted squire joined them and nodded to the platform. His visor was down so they could not see his face.

Morgan le Fay stood, silencing the crowd. Raising her hands, she screeched, "Let the tournament begin!"

Trumpets blasted and the spectators shouted their encouragement. They weren't cheering for any of the squires in particular; they were just happy to have a break from their labors.

The archery contest was first.

Dallin and Accolon's squire walked to the center of the field where everyone could see them. A large target with painted circles was fastened to a bale of hay.

Wow, one hundred paces is a lot further than I imagined, Dallin thought.

Looking down at Dallin, the squire said, "I shall destroy thee."

"Nuh uh, I'm going to destroy you," Dallin retorted, trying to sound confident. However, he was worried that Leeana had not been able to put his plan into action.

"I am Accolon's best archer," the older boy boasted. "I have never been bested by a squire."

"So? I'm the best slingshot shooter in my entire elementary school," Dallin said. "If you think you are so good, then I'll let you have the first shot."

The squire hawked a loogie, rolled it around in his mouth, and then spat it onto Dallin's boot. "Ye shall not let me have anything. I shall *take* the first shot because I am the best."

"How rude," Dallin complained, trying to shake the slimy glob of mucus from his boot.

Accolon's squire laughed, then pulled an arrow from his quiver. Dallin stopped jumping around and watched carefully so he would know what to do when it was his turn. Knocking an arrow to his bow, the squire took aim down the shaft, raised the tip of the arrow and released. The arrow arched gracefully into the air, sailing effortlessly toward the target. Nothing was going wrong, which was not part of the plan.

Thwap! The arrow hit the outer ring of the target, sinking halfway into the hay.

The squire did not hear Dallin's moan over the cheering of the crowd. Something was seriously wrong. Leeana obviously had not sabotaged the arrows.

Dallin took a deep breath, trying to calm his jittery hands.

"It's okay. I'm great with my slingshot. This bow is just a big slingshot. I can do it," he told himself.

Removing an arrow, he imitated the squire, knocked it to the bowstring, pulled back, sighted down the shaft, and released.

Twang! The arrow cut through the air, straight for the target. It did not have as much height as the squire's arrow, but Dallin had put more power behind it—he hoped. Unfortunately he had not put enough.

Laughter rolled through the crowd as Dallin's arrow nose-dived into the dirt a few paces in front of the target. He missed completely.

"Shall we call me the winner now?" the squire sneered.

Dallin furrowed his brow and said, "Again."

The squire shrugged, knocked another arrow, and let loose. Dallin held his breath, hoping that perhaps Leeana had just missed sabotaging the first arrow, but that the second arrow would wobble and miss the target.

Thwap! No such luck, another hit followed by more cheering.

Dallin prepared for his next shot. He removed the backpack from under his cloak in order to give himself better pull. This time he aimed higher, raising the point of his arrow another fifteen degrees and pulled back harder. He held his breath, and released.

Twang! The arrow shot high in the air. Dallin continued to hold his breath, watching the arrow drop. But it did not drop fast enough, and the arrow overshot the target.

More loud jeers and laughter from the crowd; Dallin could even hear the screeching laughter of Morgan le Fay. She seemed to be enjoying herself.

Dallin kicked his backpack in frustration, knocking out the roll of duct tape.

Accolon's squire laughed. "Thou shouldst give up, squire. Ye can not even hit the target."

Picking up the tape, Dallin had an idea.

"No! You give up!" he challenged. "If you shoot one more arrow you'll be sorry."

"Me, give up?" the squire asked in amazement. "Have ye not been watching? Those are my arrows in the target. Thine are in the dirt!"

"This is your last chance," Dallin said. "Give up now or be sorry."

"Ye are dead," the squire threatened, gritting his teeth. He reached into his quiver, extracted a black goose-feathered arrow, aimed and released.

While everyone was watching the squire's black arrow, Dallin reached into his backpack and pulled out his last firecracker. He ripped the tip off an arrow and quickly taped the explosive to the end. If this did not work, he was out of tricks.

Thwap! Bull's eye.

As the squire bowed to the cheering crowd, Dallin lit the fuse, knocked the arrow, aimed and released.

Twang!

Hearing Dallin's arrow leave his bow, the squire turned.

"Why dost thou even try?" the squire mocked.

Dallin ignored him, watching as his arrow peaked and then began its descent straight toward the target.

"Please don't explode too early," he pleaded.

Thwap! BOOM!

A direct hit! The arrow landed in the middle of the target and exploded, spraying the field with pieces of broken arrows and burning hay. The crowd stared in stunned silence for three long seconds, then erupted with cheers of approval. All of the squire's arrows had disintegrated; leaving Dallin's two missed arrows the only ones even near the target. Morgan le Fay stared dumbfounded at the smoldering heap.

The judges bowed their heads together in consultation. Several minutes ticked by, and Dallin began to get nervous. He looked over at Ethan who smiled encouragingly. Finally a judge broke away from the group and walked to the edge of the platform. The crowd fell silent.

"The archery winner is…" the judge yelled, "Squire Mordred!"

CHAPTER 14

Jousting Surprise

It took a second before Dallin realized that he was squire Mordred. When he did, he jumped for joy, pumping his fist in the air. The crowd roared their approval.

Accolon's squire bowed his head in shame and exited the field, back to his master's tent.

Looking away from the retreating squire, Dallin noticed Ethan and the second squire lining up at opposite ends of the field. Their horses were snorting, ready to charge. With a bugle blast, Accolon's squire thundered down the field directly toward Ethan, long brown hair flowing out from the back of his helmet.

No time to celebrate Dallin's victory, Ethan pulled down his visor and kicked his horse into action, bellowing a war cry. The sound bounced around inside his metal helmet making his ears ring.

Dallin held his breath. With his event he did not have to worry about getting hurt. But even if Ethan won the joust, he could still get seriously injured by the other squire's blunt lance if it hit him.

Ethan held a large shield in front of him with his right arm, and aimed his bouncing lance at his opponent with his left.

The crowd held their breath, waiting, waiting... and then it was over. A miss. Both squires missed their opponent, and both remained on their horses.

The crowd exhaled an "Ahh" of disappointment.

Reaching the far end of the field, Ethan and the squire each turned their horses around, their lances pointing skyward again. They lined up, and then charged.

The squire does not seem to have any problems holding his lance, Ethan thought. *Leeana must have failed.*

Focusing on the charge instead of on Leeana, Ethan tried to balance the lance on top of his shield. It helped.

CRACK!

Instead of hitting the riders, the blunt lances smashed into each other. Ethan was not prepared for the force of the crashing lances, and lost his grip. The pole flew out of his hand with a painful jerk.

The crowd cheered.   Now it was getting interesting.

Turning his horse around, dread filled Ethan's heart.

"Oh no!" he cried out. The force of the blow hadn't knocked the lance out of the other squire's hand. Instead the impact had broken the tip of his lance, turning the blunt end into a sharp spear.

Chomping at its bit, Ethan's horse was anxious to make another pass, but he held it in check while reaching for his only other weapon. If a knight looses his lance, then his other option is a flail: a wooden handle with a long chain and spiked ball.

Ethan quickly ran options through his head. *If I can wrap the chain around the squire's lance, I may be able to pull it out of his hands. But if I miss, I'll be skewered.*

Accolon's squire charged. Ethan did the same. He swung the heavy ball like a windmill, careful not to impale his own head with the spikes. As the riders drew closer, Ethan's momentum increased, and he focused on the lowering lance.

Timing it just right, Ethan swung up, wrapping the chain around the sharp end of the lance, prevented it from running him through. As they passed, Ethan pulled with all his might. Instead of pulling the lance free from his opponent's grasp, the lance jerked up yanking the flail out of Ethan's hand. The flail flew fifty feet through the air and crashed into a tent, toppling it over.

The crowd hooted and hollered, thrilled by the action.

Stunned by the loss of his flail, Ethan had no time to make a new plan before he realizing that his horse was charging again. The squire began to lower his javelin. Ethan ducked behind his shield just in time, but the tip of the broken lance caught the shield and jerked it off his arm. Pain shot through Ethan's shoulder, and he lost his concentration, dropping the horse's reigns. Realizing what had happened, he panicked and almost fell off his horse. Without the reigns, he could no longer control his horse and try to stop this madness.

The crowd cheered louder.

Following its training, the horse turned around at the end of the field and began another charge. Ethan was about to get harpooned, and there was nothing he could do about it. He needed a weapon, or something, but all he had left was his armor.

My armor! That's it.

Reaching under his chin he unstrapped the helmet, removed it from his head, and threw his first perfect spiral.

Direct hit! Ethan's helmet smashed into the oncoming squire, knocking the rider backwards over his horse. He fell to the ground with a crash, his helmet bouncing off. Despite the fall, the broken lance remained in the squire's hand, pointing skyward.

"Woo-hoo!" Ethan yelled with relief, joining in the celebration of the crowd. He pumped his fist, and the audience roared louder.

Ethan's horse trotted over to the platform where Dallin was doing his victory dance: the jumping cockroach. It looked like he was walking barefoot on hot coals while at the same time trying to wipe invisible spider webs off his face and body. Ethan released his pent-up anxiety and laughed.

The judges bowed their head in consultation, and then made their announcement.

"The jousting winner is…" the judge yelled, "Squire Mordred!"

The crowd shouted their approval. They did not care who won, but the fact that both wins had been very unconventional pleased the audience.

After a few minutes of celebration, Morgan le Fay stood and dismissed the peasants, "Everyone back to work. We have a war to prepare for."

As the people grudgingly dispersed, Morgan addressed Ethan and Dallin.

"Sir Mordred's squires have once again proven their remarkable skill," she spoke softly, looking at Ethan and Dallin with a burning glint in her evil eye. "Accolon shall escort thee back to Mordred, along with the fake Excalibur. When ye return, I have plans for thee. I see great potential in such resourceful lads."

Ethan and Dallin bowed.

"Accolon," Morgan ordered. "Get the sword from the vault and take these squires to Mordred. I expect thee to return by nightfall with more soldiers. We shall attack at first light tomorrow."

"Yes, my Queen," the giant said, smashing his closed fist to his chest with a hollow clang.

Ethan and Dallin sighed with relief. They still had to figure out how to escape before reaching Mordred, but at least they would be away from Morgan le Fay.

"Stop!" someone yelled from across the tournament field.

Turning, they saw Accolon's squire, the one who lost the arrow competition. He staggered out of his tent. A second squire leaned on his arm, struggling to walk due to the fact that his legs were tied together.

"Stop!" he cried again. "The rider is an imposter."

Hearing the commotion, the rider Ethan had knocked down while jousting slowly rose to her feet and then struggled back onto the horse, broken lance still in hand. Without a helmet, the rider was easily recognizable. The light olive skin and flowing brown hair instantly gave her away.

"It's Leeana," Dallin said in surprise.

"Wha-what? How?" Ethan stammered.

"That girl!" Morgan screeched. "She is Lancelot's daughter. Crush her!"

Accolon instantly obeyed. He jumped off the platform with amazing speed despite all his armor, and rushed the girl.

Leeana's horse saw the oncoming foe, reared up on its hind legs, and charged. The Black Knight ran almost as fast as the horse, metal legs pounding over the ground like a steam locomotive.

"Leeana, look out!" Ethan screamed as man and beast were about to collide.

Accolon jumped twenty feet into the air, hurtling directly for Leeana.

"Impossible," Dallin mumbled.

Throwing her arm up defensively, the broken lance whipped through the air and caught the knight in the shoulder, piercing his metal armor. The lance splintered into pieces, and the knight crumpled to the ground in a heap of twisted metal. Accolon's cauldron helmet hit the ground and rolled away, revealing an empty space where the head should have been.

Leeana's horse staggered, but managed to stay upright. A tremor ran through the knight, but he did not get up.

"No! My precious Black Knight!" Morgan wailed.

"Dallin, grab on." Ethan spurred his horse forward, reached for his brother's extended hand, and swung him up. They rode over to Leeana who remained staring at the fallen Black Knight.

"Leeana, let's go!" Ethan yelled.

"Wait," she said, watching the heap of metal move.

From the hole beneath the helmet, first one, and then two scrawny arms wiggled out. Following the arms, a gaunt old man with a long gray beard wormed out of the massive chest cavity like a hermit crab abandoning its shell. He stood on unsteady feet, and looked around. Smoke began to rise from the empty armor, and black oil leaked from the punctured shoulder.

"Ye have saved me!" the old man cried, clasping his hands together and falling to his knees.

CHAPTER 15

Dumlin the Dunderhead

"Seize them!" Morgan le Fay bellowed, leading her knights and soldiers in a charge across the field. "Do not let them escape!"

The mists that had lingered at the edges of the tournament field surged forward, following Morgan le Fay.

"Play time is over," Ethan said, spurring his horse away from the advancing soldiers.

Jumping in front of Leeana's horse, the old man grabbed the reins and begged, "Please, take me with thee."

"Why should I?" Leeana said, trying to break free. "Ye tried to kill me."

"Please! I was under a spell!" Pointing to the pile of metal, he begged, "Ye must take me with thee or I shall be forced back into that…that machine."

Unable to gain control of her horse with the wild man hanging on, she extended her hand. "Hasten and mount up! I hope I shall not regret this."

He scrambled up behind her, and the horse bolted away from the advancing Morgan le Fay.

"Shoot them! Shoot them!" she screamed. "They know about Excalibur!"

Fortunately, no one had brought any other horses to the tournament field, though several knights had bows. Arrows began whizzing toward them.

Twisting to face the rear of the horse, the old man chanted, "Contego Presidium Defendo!"

Looking over her shoulder, Leeana saw a shimmering blue light behind them. Arrows bounced harmlessly off of it.

"Are ye a magician?" Leeana asked.

"No, I am a scientist. But I am familiar with a fair share of magical charms."

Seeing that their arrows could not hit Leeana and the old man, the archers aimed further down field, and began shooting at Ethan and Dallin. Fortunately they were already out of range.

Glancing over her shoulder one last time, Leeana saw the squire that had lost to Dallin in the archery contest. A black arrow left his bow, and Leeana watched it arch over them.

"NO!" she screamed. "Dallin, watch out!"

Too late. Just as Ethan and Dallin were about to disappear over a hill, the arrow struck home, sinking into Dallin's back.

It was Leeana's turn to beg. "Please, old man, tell me that ye know some healing magic."

"Alas, I am no good at healing. The last time I tried, I nearly blew up the patient."

Streaking through the mists, Leeana charged after the boys. They where were just about to enter the grove of trees where, earlier in the day, they had tied their own mounts.

By the time Leeana had caught up and entered the grove, the dapple charger Ethan had jousted with was now riderless, a pile of armor at its feet. The boys had abandoned Morgan le Fay's horse and were mounting their own horses from Leeana's stables.

"Help me, Ethan," Dallin yelled.

Ethan was already on the back of his brown horse, while Dallin struggled to climb up onto his black stallion, heedless of the arrow lodged between his shoulder blades.

"Dallin, stop! Ye are hurt," Leeana yelled, surprised that he was not writhing in pain on the ground. She jumped off her charger to help, but crashed to the ground under the weight of her armor.

"Huh?" Dallin said, looking around. He rushed over to help Leeana get up.

"Oh no!" Ethan yelled, seeing the arrow sticking out of his brother's back for the first time. "Dallin, you've been shot."

Pulling Leeana up off the ground, Dallin looked over his shoulder. Shocked to see an arrow sticking out of his back, he let go of Leeana and she promptly teetered and fell back again.

"Ahhh! I'm dead!" Dallin wailed.

"I think not," the old man said. He jumped off the horse and yanked the arrow out of Dallin's back

"Hey, I didn't feel a thing!" Dallin exclaimed.

"I thought ye could not heal him," Leeana said, staring at the bearded man.

"I did not heal him," the man smiled, his eyes twinkling.

"But then…how?"

He lifted Dallin's cloak, revealing the backpack underneath. There was a small hole where the arrow

had punctured it. Opening the bag, Dallin pulled out a thick chunk of waxy ambergris with an arrow hole most of the way through it.

"Ha, ha!" Ethan laughed. "I can see the headlines now: 'Boy Saved by Whale Vomit.'"

Dallin laughed too. Leeana and the old man looked at each other in confusion. They didn't know that the waxy blob Dallin held in his hands was ambergris—solidified whale vomit—obtained on their previous traveling trunk adventure in Atlantis.

Putting the backpack on, Dallin handed his cloak to the old man. "Here, I think you need this more than me." All the old man had on was a ratty pair of long underpants.

"Oh, I thank thee. 'Tis a bit chilly without my metal suit."

"Speaking of which," Ethan said, "What exactly were you doing inside that robot, pretending to be Sir Accolon?"

"I was not pretending to be Sir Accolon. I am Sir Accolon, at your service," the man said, thumping his bony chest with a clenched fist.

Removing her heavy armor, Leeana said in disbelief, "*Ye* are Sir Accolon?"

"Well, yes, in a manner of speaking," he said. "Over a decade ago I was hired by Morgan le Fay to create a mechanical suit that wouldst look like a knight. The end result was A.C.L.O.N.: Advanced Cyborg that Learns, Organizes and is Nice—more commonly known as Sir Accolon."

"What's with the 'nice' part?" Dallin said. "You sure weren't nice when you were inside that robot."

"True, true, and I hope thou wilt forgive me," the old man said. "Knowing of Morgan's famed cruelty, I built in some preventive measures that would keep the machine from doing anything mean. After climbing inside and demonstrating the machine's power and abilities, Morgan cast a spell on me, forcing me to be her slave. The first thing she did was force me to get rid of the robot's nice programming. The last ten years have been a nightmare. I was compelled by her dark magic to obey her every command. Not until thou didst knock me down was the spell finally broken."

Bowing to Leeana, he said, "Again, I thank thee for saving me. Now, shall we go?"

"Wait a minute," Ethan said. "Who are you really, and why should we trust you?"

"My apologies for not properly introducing myself. Living in a metal shell hast made me forget my manners." Puffing out his scrawny chest, he announced, "I am Dumlin the Scientist, younger brother to Merlin the Wizard."

"Merlin has a brother?" Leeana said in shock; though now that he mentioned it, she could see the family resemblance.

"Yes, well, the family doth not talk about me much," Dumlin said sheepishly, his beard drooping. "They did not believe in science or my pursuit of its study. 'Ye must learn to be a good magician like thine older brother,' my mother would tell me. 'Science is a bunch of hocus-pocus. Nothing useful shall ever come of it,' my father used to say."

Sighing, he continued, "I did not listen. I gave up on magic and began to experiment, but nothing worked the way I imagined. Merlin and his friends teased me, calling me names like Dumlin the Dunce, Dumlin the Nincompoop, and my least favorite, Dumlin the Dunderhead. Then after a little accident—well, um, maybe not so little accident—I was driven out of the village, or what was left of it.

I travelled around the country, earning my living by fixing broken wheels or mending cracked ovens. In my spare time I invented things."

"Like what kinds of things?" Ethan asked.

"Oh, the most amazing gadgets," Dumlin said, excited to have someone show interest. "I created a glass bulb that can trap light, and glow all night long. It is a marvel to behold. I call it the glowing-bulb-of-harnessed-lightening. Pretty catchy name, wouldn't ye agree?"

"Uh, yeah," Dallin shrugged. "We have those at home. We call them light bulbs."

"Ooo, 'light bulbs.' I like it," Dumlin said. "Well, Morgan le Fay heard of my abilities and hired me to create a mechanical knight for her. The rest is, shall we say, history."

Wailing shrieks filled the air as thick tendrils of mist crept into the grove of trees.

"Uh, I think it's time to go," Ethan said.

"Right ye are," Dumlin agreed, assisting Dallin up. "Let's ride."

CHAPTER 16

Isen~Draca

The long ride back to Camelot allowed them to get a few things straight about Leeana's involvement in the tournament. After they were well away from Castle deOrk and the wailing mists, Leeana explained. When she was unable to find and sabotage any arrows, she turned her attention to the lance. The jouster, however, had planned a few tricks of his own. His lance was permanently attached to his armor, which would give him a clear advantage over Ethan. Since she couldn't pour sunblock on the handle to make it slippery, she waited for the squire, knocked him out, tied him up, and then took his place.

"No wonder you never lost hold of your lance," Ethan said. "And here I was thinking that you were the strongest girl in the world."

"I did hope that if our lances collided, mine would be knocked free and thou couldst win the tournament," Leeana said. "I underestimated the squire's treachery. Even thy courageous act to coil thy flail around my lance failed to pull it free. T'was a good thing thou thought to throw thy helmet at me. It would have looked suspicious if I fell off my horse without cause."

"If the archer hadn't gone into the tent and found the tied-up squire, everything would have turned out just fine," said Dallin.

"We are indeed fortunate to have escaped," Leeana concluded.

"Hear, hear," Dumlin agreed.

After a pause, Ethan asked, "So what are we going to do now?"

"I say we just go to King Arthur and tell him the truth," Dallin said.

Ethan shook his head. "I don't think the king will believe us without proof. If only we had been able to get Morgan's fake sword."

Dumlin coughed, clearing his throat. "If I may be of assistance, I shall gladly tell Arthur that ye speak the truth."

"Thanks, but is he going to believe you?" Ethan asked. "After all, you were Sir Accolon for the last ten years."

"Thy point is well made."

"I believe Merlin to be the answer," Leeana said. "We shall explain the situation to him, and he can advise the king. After all, Merlin is the one who sent thee here."

"Do you think he will have anything for us to eat?" Dallin asked.

"I sure hope so," Ethan said. "That cheese is not sitting well with my stomach."

Leeana raised her hand for silence. "Do ye hear that?"

The riders cocked their heads, listening.

"Something approacheth."

Reining in the horses, they turned to look behind them. The wind began to blow in short gusts, bending the treetops with a rhythmic whoosh, whoosh, whoosh. The horses whinnied, clopping their hooves nervously.

"It's just the wind," said Dallin.

Dumlin anxiously scanned the sky. Focusing his attention on the horizon, he mumbled, "Tis Isen-Draca."

"Who is Isen-Draca?" Dallin asked.

"Iron-Dragon," Leeana interpreted from the old tongue. "But there is no such thing as dragons."

Dumlin pointed over the treetops, his hand trembling.

A black spot appeared on the horizon, growing larger with every gust of wind. The speck tore through the air on two massive, leathery wings, revealing an armor-plated body with four metal legs and multiple tails made from long chains with spiked balls at their ends.

As the metal dragon spotted the riders, two burning yellow eyes flared in the late afternoon sky. One eye was larger than the other. As it drew closer, the larger eye appeared to be in the center of the dragon's head, which meant the smaller eye belonged to the rider: Morgan le Fay.

"Attack!" the sorceress commanded.

The dragon opened its maw and uttered a metallic screech. It tucked its wings in and dove for the kill.

"RUN!" Dumlin cried.

The horses didn't need any encouragement.

Hurtling toward them like an iron comet, the dragon opened its mouth and belched a ball of fire. The road in front of Leeana erupted in flames. Instinctively her horse leapt over the burning pothole, singeing its belly hair. The rest of the riders maneuvered around the geyser of flames, trying to stay together.

The mechanical monster spread its wings, gliding just above the heads of the fleeing riders. The spiked balls at the end of the chain-tails swung through the air creating a deadly obstacle course. It took all of their concentration to dodge the flying flails and not fall from their horses.

Reaching the front rider, the dragon lowered its head, stretching its neck as it reached for Leeana. The metallic jaws opened wide enough to bite the girl in half.

Hearing the grinding of gears, Leeana looked over her shoulder, and frantically jerked the reins hard to the left. Her horse hurtled recklessly off the road and into the undergrowth as the iron jaws snapped shut. The dragon missed her by mere inches, getting a mouthful of tree branches instead.

The other riders plunged into the undergrowth behind Leeana. Morgan pulled the dragon skyward and circled for a second assault.

"How did Morgan get an iron dragon?" Leeana cried, desperately trying to avoid tree branches.

"I made it," Dumlin confessed. "But I could never get Isen-Draca to stay in the air. The machine was too top heavy and would always crash head first."

"Then how is it flying now?" Dallin cried out. He glanced up through the trees as Morgan passed overhead, emitting another earsplitting screech.

"The tails," Dumlin pointed. "It's brilliant. She must have added the balls and chains as a counterweight to keep the machine balanced."

"Yeah, that's brilliant and all, but how do we stop it?" Ethan demanded.

"The only way to stop the dragon is to destroy— look out!"

Morgan swooped down, plunging in a head-on collision course at a frightening speed. The chain-tails dragged through the trees like a giant weedwhacker, cutting a wide path through the forest. A sapling exploded in front of Ethan, filling the air with a million splinters as a spiked ball flew at his head. He reacted by pushed against the horse's neck, throwing himself into a backward somersault off the back of his horse. Tumbling through the air the ball swung over his head, the lowest spike grazing his eyebrow.

Leeana and Dallin veered to either side of the destructive tail, letting the dragon pass before halting their horses. Turning around, they saw Ethan under a pile of splintered tree branches, but Dumlin was nowhere to be seen.

Dismounting, Dallin ran over to Ethan and pulled him out of the path of destruction.

"You okay, Ethan?"

"Yeah," he gasped. "Just got the wind knocked out of me."

"Your eyebrow," Dallin said, pointing. "It's bleeding."

Ethan raised his hand and gingerly touched his brow. "Ouch. I thought things looked a little blurry."

Wiping the blood from his forehead and eye, he surveyed the scene. Trees and branches littered the path cleared by the dragon's tail. Several trees had spiked balls embedded in their trunks, sap oozing from their injuries. Morgan was nowhere to be seen, but no doubt she was patrolling the sky with Isen-Draca. Ethan's horse had run off, and Dumlin was still missing. As soon as Morgan found them, they would be in serious trouble.

"Can you see okay?"

"Yes, I can see fine," Ethan said, and then paused. "That's it!"

"What's it?"

"I can see. That's the answer."

"What answer?" Dallin asked, totally confused.

"That is how we stop Morgan!" Ethan said excitedly. "The iron-dragon's eye is yellow, just like Morgan's evil eye. That must be how she controls it. Dumlin was saying we needed to destroy something to stop Morgan and the dragon, but he never finished. I bet it's the eye. Where is he? Where's Dumlin?"

"Over here," Leeana called, removing a pile of broken branches from off his limp body.

Ethan and Dallin rushed over. If it hadn't been for the large lump on his forehead, the boys might have thought the old man was taking a nap.

Ethan checked for a pulse.

"Is he alive?" Dallin asked nervously.

"Yes, he's just unconscious."

"Great," Dallin sighed, "Now how are we going to know if you're right?"

"I must be right. Besides, what other option do we have? Even if it doesn't stop Morgan, we can at least try to blind the machine and make a run for it."

Looking around nervously, Leeana said, "Why hast Morgan not attacked again?"

Ethan pointed at the spiked balls in the trees. "If what Dumlin said is true, without all of her counterweights she is probably having a hard time flying."

"Okay, even if you *are* right about the eye, how do we destroy it?" Dallin asked.

"Do you have any more firecrackers? You could light one and shoot it at the dragon's eye with your slingshot"

Dallin shook his head no. "We've used them all up."

Grabbing Dumlin by the legs, Ethan said, "I don't know then, but we've got to keep moving. Help me put Dumlin on Leeana's horse. She can carry him and I'll ride with you."

Securing Dumlin and Leeana on her horse, Ethan mounted Dallin's black charger and lowered a hand to help him up.

As Dallin reached for Ethan's hand, the horse whinnied, rearing up on its hind legs.

"Whoa!" Ethan yelled, clinging to its mane.

Eyes wide with fear, the horse almost kicked Dallin in the head before charging into the forest, taking Ethan with it. Leeana's horse panicked and followed close behind.

"Hey, wait for me!" Dallin screamed. He watched helplessly as Leeana and Ethan disappeared into the trees, the clopping hooves growing faint as they got farther and farther away until all was silent.

A moment later the silence was shattered by a deafening roar as Isen-Draca and its rider crash-landed into the clearing, sending up a hail of leaves and sticks. Dallin was blown backwards by the hurricane gale created by the dragon's powerful wings. As he tumbled, his backpack snagged a broken tree limb, wrenching the zipper open, and scattering the contents.

Scrambling to his feet, Dallin stepped on his fallen slingshot. Hearing the growl of grinding gears behind him, Dallin slid his foot underneath the weapon and slowly turned around. The massive metal dragon crouched thirty feet away, steam rising from its joints. Morgan le Fay crouched on its back, the yellow light in her eye pulsing in sync with the dragon's cyclopic eye.

"It appears that like thy friends have abandoned thee, boy. Not to worry, I shall destroy them as soon as I am done with thee," Morgan promised. "Isen-Draca, attack!"

The dragon tucked its wings and pounced. Dallin kicked his slingshot into the air, snatched it with his right hand and cart wheeled away from the snapping jaws. His left hand grabbed a smooth stone off the ground as he finished his cartwheel, and he landed with the elastic bands pulled taut.

The machine recoiled from its first attack and then lunged a second time as Dallin released the loaded slingshot. Stone and dragon eye collided five feet in front of Dallin's face.

Morgan le Fay's cry of pain mingled with the tinkling of shattered glass as the dragon's eye exploded in a burst of bright yellow flames. Morgan toppled backwards, holding her head as she writhed in pain on the ground. Isen-Draca pitched forward, metallic teeth oozing flaming drops of oil. It teetered, swaying slowly, and then crumpled in a heap of smoking metal at Dallin's feet.

He didn't wait to see if Morgan, or the dragon, would get back up. Sprinting for the tree line, he heard horse hooves approaching fast.

Ethan burst through a tangle of trees, Leeana close behind.

"Grab my hand," Ethan shouted.

Taking a running leap off a fallen tree, Dallin seized his brother's outstretched hand, and swung up onto the back of the galloping horse.

CHAPTER 17

Cream puffs

Dumlin was conscious by the time they reached Merlin's house.

"Hello? Anyone here?" Ethan shouted, knocking for the third time.

Still no answer.

"Come," Dumlin said, pushing open the door. "Merlin is bound to have some healing balm for thine eyebrow and my bruised head."

The cottage was a disaster, as if it had been hit by a hurricane.

"Oh no, we're too late," Dallin said. "It looks like someone got here before us and destroyed Merlin's house."

"Hogwash," Dumlin said. "My brother never had any organizational sense. Growing up, his bedroom always looked like this."

Besides smelling strange—
like peppermint sticks and
vinegar—the cottage was packed
full of bizarre artifacts. The walls
were hung with tapestries, maps,
and ferocious tribal masks. Grungy
books, dust-filled urns, scrolls, and

tablets of stone were piled everywhere throughout the house, except on the shelves. The shelves were reserved for jars of bizarre plants and animals floating in different colored liquids. Thin trails between the mounds of clutter led deeper into the house.

"We should spread out and see if we can find Merlin in this mess," Dumlin said.

Dallin wandered through several rooms before he reached the back of the cottage and spotted something worth looking for: food. On a crowded work table between piles of books, rags and bottles, lay a platter of small round pastries oozing colorful puffs of cream. Reaching for a dark-green pastry with lime-green cream, Dallin accidentally bumped a tall stack of books, sending them cascading off the side of the overloaded table. Grabbing at the books he tried to balance them, but that only made matters worse, sending more precariously stacked items over the edge. Giving up, he snatched the pastry platter, held it high, and waited for the piles to stop falling.

Books, bottles, pots and pans crashed onto the floor, making the room even messier than it was before, if that were possible. Finally everything stopped moving, and Dallin put the platter down, stuffing the green pastry into his mouth.

"Mmm, delicious," he mumbled, his mouth full of pastry. "Ethan, come here, you've got to try one of these."

Ethan walked into the room perusing a book of magic.

"Sweet! Cream puffs!" Putting the book aside he chose an orange and blue one. With the pastry halfway to his mouth, he stopped abruptly. "Dallin, your skin is turning green!"

Dallin looked down at his arms. "What? Ahh! What's happening to me?" he yelped. Multiple shades of green were crawling across his arms in a zigzag pattern.

Dumlin stumbled into the room wearing some of Merlin's robes, oblivious to Dallin's peril, or the enormous mess. "Here Ethan, I didst find some healing balm." Dabbing yellow paste on Ethan's eyebrow, the cut healed instantly. He capped the vial and tucked it into Ethan's tunic. "In case ye need some more later."

When Ethan failed to pay him any attention, Dumlin realized something was wrong. Noticing Ethan's wide eyes staring across the room, he turned around and gaped at Dallin. Then he began to chuckle. Dallin's skin was a pale lime color with dark-green stripes zigzagging up the exposed parts of his body. He looked like a giant, human watermelon.

"What luck! I have not had one of Merlin's color-changing cream puffs for decades," Dumlin said, popping a purple and yellow pastry into his mouth. "They are very tasty, and were always a big hit at the balls and banquets."

Dumlin slowly turned bright purple with yellow zebra stripes. "Not to worry, the effect wears off as soon as ye burp."

Dallin let out a gigantic burp and a puff of green air escaped from his mouth. His color instantly began to fade.

"Awesome!" Dallin said, stuffing another cream puff into his mouth.

Ethan popped the one he was holding into his mouth and watched his skin turn bright orange with blue polka dots.

"Ahh!" Leeana cried, walking into the room. "Ye have all been cursed."

After explaining the treats to Leeana, they spent the next twenty minutes eating all of Merlin's color-changing cream puffs and burping up a storm. They were laughing so hard they did not hear the clinking of armor as soldiers surrounded the cottage.

"Well, we better come up with a new plan," Ethan said after all the tasty pastries were gone. "We can't just wait at Merlin's house all day."

"Why not?" Dallin asked. "Maybe we can find more treats if we look through the cupboards."

Dumlin agreed whole-heartedly. "And while ye are at it, look for something to quench an old man's thirs—"

"Seize them!" an armored knight yelled, bursting through the cottage's back door.

CHAPTER 18

The Round Table

Surrounded by knights with drawn swords, King Arthur made his way into the messy cottage.

Facing Dumlin, who was chocolate-brown with hot-pink rings circling his body, the king demanded, "Who art thou?"

"BELCH!" Dumlin burped quite rudely, releasing a brown-pink cloud into Arthur's face. Ethan and Dallin snickered. "Apologies my Lord, I could not keep that gas in any longer. I am Dumlin, younger brother to Merlin."

"Well, where is thy brother?" the king asked, waving away the colorful cloud. "I came to consult with him and I find thee having a party with Morgan le Fay's spies."

"Sir, we are not spies," Ethan said. "We bring you good news. Morgan le Fay does not have Excalibur.

She only has a fake sword and is using it to try and rally troops."

Facing Ethan, the king said, "Why should I believe thee? Thou couldst be leading me into a trap."

"It is no trap, your Majesty," Leeana said. "We speak the truth. Merlin sent them here to help thee. We only scarcely returned from Castle deOrk, having discovered that Morgan le Fay heard of the missing Excalibur and created a false one in order to raise an army against thee."

"Ye returned from Castle deOrk?" King Arthur said, visibly impressed. "No one has ever returned from Morgan's castle and still had their wits about them. Did ye see the fake Excalibur?"

The three companions looked at each other, and shook their heads no.

"Well, then how do ye know it is a counterfeit? And if she hath a fake, then why is the real Excalibur still missing? Until my sword is returned, thou shalt all remain in the dungeon. Guarded this time!"

Waving to his guards, King Arthur ordered, "Tie them up."

"No, please. Ye must ask Merlin," Leeana cried, backing away from the knights. "Find Merlin!"

"Merlin! Merlin!" Ethan and Dallin yelled together.

"Merlin, where art thou?" Dumlin bellowed, adding to the noise.

"Oi! What's all the ruckus? Who is calling me?" an old, gray-bearded man said, popping his head in through an open window. "Goodness me, your Majesty. What is everyone doing here?"

"Merlin, thou hast returned," Leeana cried out in joy.

"Returned? Me returned? Why, I never departed," the old man said. "The only jaunt I've had today was to the out-house. I read a chapter or two from the latest edition of *Medieval Marvels*, and must have forgotten about the time. Wonderful read, *Medieval Marvels*. There is a fantastic spell in here that turns warts into—"

He was about to open the book when King Arthur interrupted. "Merlin, stop rambling and get thyself in here. Excalibur is missing and war is upon our threshold. There is much to discuss."

"Yes, your Majesty. Right away, sire."

As Merlin stumbled through the back door, King Arthur said, "Now we shall have the truth."

"Yes, your Majesty. What service may I perform for thee?" Merlin asked, placing *Medieval Marvels* on a teetering pile of pots.

"Tell me, Merlin, dost thou know these people?" the king asked.

Merlin looked over his round spectacles at Ethan, Dallin, Leeana and Dumlin.

"Well sir, I am well acquainted with Leeana, daughter of Lancelot," Merlin began. "And that old codger over there, why I do believe that is my younger brother Dumlin. Is that really you Dummy? Why, brother, where hast thou been these many long years?"

"Merlin, ye remember me!" Dumlin said, embracing his brother.

"Remember thee? Of course I remember thee. How could anyone ever forget the brother who almost blew up the entire village," Merlin chuckled.

"What about these squires," King Arthur directed, trying to bring the conversation back to business.

"What? Are those some of Mordred's squires? No, I do not know them. I have never seen them before."

"Ah-ha! Spies—just as I suspected," the king boomed.

"No," Leeana cried out. "Ethan and Dallin are not spies. Merlin, did ye not tell me this morning that everything would be well with my father and that I should return home?"

"Yes, I remember telling thee that."

"Upon my return, Ethan and Dallin had magically appeared inside my father's armory. Thy magic brought them here to find the King's lost sword."

"What? No, I never use magic to summon people," Merlin said. "And what is this hubbub about Excalibur being lost? Tis not lost, I have it right here on my—"

Merlin looked at the messy table.

"It's gone. Excalibur is gone!" Merlin exclaimed.

"Of course it is gone," King Arthur said. "And I've thrown Lancelot in the dungeon for its disappearance."

"No, no, no. I had the sword right here on my table and *now* it is gone," Merlin said, frantically looking around.

"What dost thou mean ye had it right here on this table?" King Arthur asked. "Are ye telling me that *thou* took it from House Lancelot?"

"Today is the day I always clean Excalibur," Merlin said, befuddled. "Once a year I conjure Excalibur to my cottage, clean it up a bit, and then return it to your secret storage place inside the large trunk at Lancelot's armory. Thou didst not think the sword stayed so nice and shiny all by itself now, didst thou?"

"Well now, I just, uh, thought it was magic," King Arthur mumbled.

"Magic, blah! Magic can't do everything. Someone has to take care of it or it shall rust. Now where did I put that sword?" After looking around the room one more time, Merlin removed his hat from his head and peered into it. "Perhaps I put it in here," he mumbled, plunging first his arm, then his head and then half his body into the pointy hat.

Looking at the mess he had made of Merlin's table, Dallin remembered hearing several metallic clangs as everything fell to the floor. Glancing behind the table, he saw a sword hilt protruding from a mound of upturned books.

Leaning over to his brother, Dallin whispered, "Ethan, I think I know where the sword is."

"You do? Where?"

Dallin nodded his head behind the table, his eyes shifting repeatedly to the sword hilt. Ethan's face lit up, and he winked at his brother.

Dallin knew that when his brother winked, he had something up his sleeve. Dallin hoped it was a wonderful idea. He was out of sunblock, firecrackers, and had lost his flashlight. He did not want to go back into the dungeon.

With a serious look on his face, Ethan said, "King Arthur, if Dallin and I can tell you where *Merlin* misplaced Excalibur, will you grant us a request?"

Looking at Ethan suspiciously, the king said, "Tell me thy request first."

"All I ask is that you free Lancelot from all charges of treason and let Leeana and my brother and I go."

"That is all? Ye do not want half my kingdom?"

"What would we do with half of your kingdom?" Dallin asked. "We have a hard enough time taking care of our bedroom."

"Very well. I shall grant thee thy wish if ye can deliver me Excalibur," Arthur declared.

"Oh, and one more thing," Dallin added. "Give Dumlin a place where he can invent things."

"Agreed," the king nodded.

"Oh, joy!" Dumlin said, smashing his scrawny fist into his open palm. "Ow, that hurts."

"Just make sure it is far away from the castle, your Highness," Merlin added. "We don't want him blowing up Camelot."

Dumlin smiled sheepishly.

"Go get it, Dallin," Ethan said.

Crawling under the table, Dallin retrieved a heavy sword. The handle was richly adorned with precious stones, the blade inscribed with mystical gold lettering.

"Ahh! There it is," Merlin said, taking the sword from Dallin. Handing it to King Arthur, Merlin said, "Here she is. Excalibur, all shiny and clean."

As King Arthur took Excalibur from Merlin, blue light emanated from the blade, lighting the room. Arthur smiled as he slid the sword into its ornate scabbard, extinguishing the light.

Kneeling before Ethan, Dallin and Leeana, the king said, "Leeana, I owe thee, thy family, and these young squires my apologies. I shall immediately free thy father from prison, and restore him as the chief Knight of the Square Table."

"That reminds me," Ethan interrupted. "One more thing your Majesty; you have got to change your square table to a round one."

"Why shouldst I do that? I happen to like the square table."

"King Arthur and the Knights of the Round Table sounds so much cooler," Dallin said.

"The king is no better than the knights who serve him," Ethan added. "Instead of a square table with the king at the head sitting on a fancy chair, a round table makes everyone equal. I once heard it said that the greatest person in a kingdom is the one who serves the people best, not the man who sits highest on the throne."

"Knights of the Round Table," King Arthur muttered, thinking it over. "Yes. Yes, I think I like that."

Removing Excalibur from its scabbard, King Arthur stood in front of Ethan and Dallin, bathing them in blue light. "Squire Ethan and Squire Dallin, ye are truly noble gentlemen. As King of Camelot, I hereby anoint thee Sir Ethan…" King Arthur tapped Excalibur lightly on Ethan and Dallin's shoulders, "And Sir Dallin, Knights of the soon-to-be Round Table.

"Come, let us make haste to the castle and free Sir Lancelot. Tonight we shall celebrate the return of Excalibur and the knighting of Sir Ethan and Sir Dallin."

Sir Kay hoisted Dallin onto his shoulders and Sir Percival lifted up Ethan. Leeana declined a hoisting.

"Three cheers for Sir Ethan, Sir Dallin and Lady Leeana," King Arthur cried.

"Hip, hip, hurrah! Hip, hip, hurrah! Hip, hip, hurrah!"

As the heroes were carried out of Merlin's cottage, Ethan yelled to Dallin, "You ready to go home now?"

"Are you kidding me? No way! Not till the party is over."

CHAPTER 19

Flash-torch

"What an adventure!" Dallin said, climbing out of the traveling trunk. "I can't wait for the next one."

"I sure hope we get a few days to rest first," Ethan said, collapsing on their big, blue LuvSac beanbag. He patted his full belly, grateful they had stuck around for the party.

Dallin hung up his backpack. "It was a good thing we went prepared."

"Sure was. Though I'm sorry I lost your flashlight."

"That's okay. At least the moat monster didn't eat me."

"Speaking of eating things, I wish we had more of Merlin's color-changing cream puffs," Ethan said.

"Ah man, we should have asked Merlin for the recipe. Then Mom could have made them for us anytime. Just think how cool it would have been to bring some of those to school."

"That would have been awesome."

A quick knock was followed by the opening of their bedroom door. Holding their little sister in one arm and a picnic basket in his other, their dad said, "I'm taking Kaitlyn to Griffith Park to ride the carousel. You boys want to come?"

Ethan and Dallin looked at each other

"I don't think we want to ride on the carousel," Ethan said.

"Yeah, we've done enough horseback riding today."

Their dad raised an eyebrow. "Well, okay. Then grab a football. I'll meet you at the car."

Reluctantly climbing off the LuvSac, Ethan crossed over to the traveling trunk—which was now just a toy chest—and opened it up to find their football. "Hey, Dallin, your flashlight is back!"

"Really? Let me see."

Ethan handed Dallin his flashlight, the one he had thrown at the moat monster. Wrapped around the flashlight was a letter.

Sir Ethan & Sir Dallin,

Life has not been as exciting since ye returned home through the enchanted trunk. I besought King Arthur for permission to retrieve thy magic light from the moat. He considered it an honor and instructed Merlin to transform the moat monster into a mermaid while we searched. We had a grand time, and Lady Guinevere taught me how to swim. The queen said I reminded her of herself, and we have quickly become close companions.

After several days of searching we found thy light. Unfortunately the magic had expired, but Merlin and Dumlin mended it by combining a little science and magic of their own. As Dallin would say, now it is cool! Though what I truly mean is that it is hot! Very hot! Be careful. I hope that every time ye use thy magic light it reminds thee of thy friends here in Camelot.

Faithfully yours,

Leeana

Post Script: On the back is the recipe for Merlin's color-changing cream puffs. Dumlin thought ye might enjoy more.

Merlin's Color-Changing Cream Puffs

Pastry Ingredients
- 1 Cup water
- ½ Cup lard
- 1 Cup flour
- ¼ Cup sugar
- ¼ Teaspoon salt
- 4 Eggs

Filling Ingredients
- ¾ Cup sugar
- 5 Tablespoons flour
- 2 Cups fresh milk
- 2 Egg yolks, beaten
- 1 Teaspoon vanilla
- A dash of salt

Magical Ingredients
- Burping Chameleon
- List of Magic Words

Pastry Preparation: Boil water in a cauldron. Add lard. Sift flour, sugar and salt to get the bugs out; add to boiling mixture and beat heartily. Remove from fire. Add eggs, stirring vigorously until smooth. Drop spoonfuls of batter onto a metal shield smeared in pig's fat. Bake in an enchanted oven at 425° for 25 minutes, until pastry is golden brown. Cool completely.

Filling Preparation: Combine sugar, flour, and salt in a knight's helmet. Stir in milk. Whisk in egg yolks. Place helmet over a cauldron of boiling water and cook until smooth but thick, stirring constantly. After 10 minutes remove helmet and cool, stirring occasionally. Add vanilla. Slit cooled cream puffs like ye would gut a fish, then stuff with cooled filling.

Magical Transformation: A chameleon must burp on each filled cream puff while ye chant the magic words for two different colors and one pattern.

Colors:
- Black: Blæc
- Blue: Næss
- Brown: Brodor
- Green: Grædig
- Orange: Lorang
- Pink: Meodfah
- Purple: Feormynd

Patterns:
- Checkers: Cefyllan
- Diamonds: Dozenge
- Polka-dots: Gæstlic
- Rings: Aþþumgyfa
- Splotches: Burnsele
- Squiggles: Eorþtilþ
- Stripes: Ongyrwan

Ethan's Guide to Medieval Armor

Medieval knights wore chain mail as their main protection. But since arrows and spears could still pierce the chain mail, knights began to add plates of steel to protect themselves. The plates were separate pieces, joined together by straps of leather. This allowed the knights to move about more freely.

A full suit of armor weighed between 50 and 100 pounds. Add on weapons and a shield and the knight might be carrying an extra 125 pounds. It was even worse for the horse that had to carry the knight plus its own armor.

A full suit of armor cost a fortune, so only the richest knights, princes and kings had   custom-made suits. Most knights wore a combination of chain mail with a few pieces of steel armor for extra protection.

Here are some examples of armor and weapons that were popular between 1200 and 1400 AD.

ARMOR

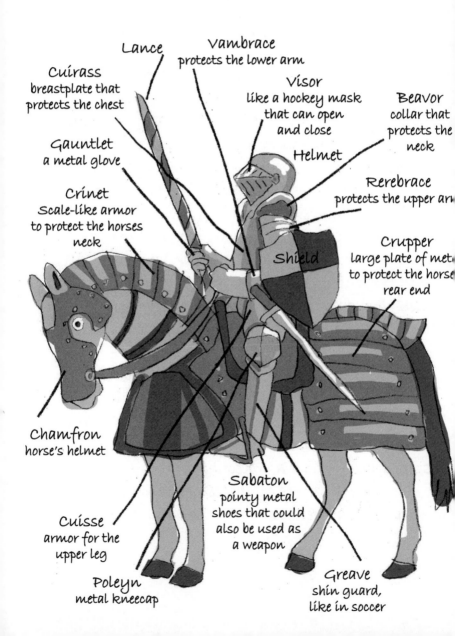

Lance

Vambrace
protects the lower arm

Cuirass
breastplate that
protects the chest

Visor
like a hockey mask
that can open
and close

Beavor
collar that
protects the
neck

Gauntlet
a metal glove

Helmet

Rerebrace
protects the upper arm

Crinet
Scale-like armor
to protect the horses
neck

Crupper
large plate of metal
to protect the horses
rear end

Shield

Chamfron
horse's helmet

Sabaton
pointy metal
shoes that could
also be used as
a weapon

Cuisse
armor for the
upper leg

Greave
shin guard,
like in soccer

Poleyn
metal kneecap

MEDIEVAL KNIGHTS

Sir Kuss of Barnum   Sir Loin of Bovine   Sir Dean of Akan

HELMETS

The Bird Brain   Canned Spinach   The Toilet Bowl

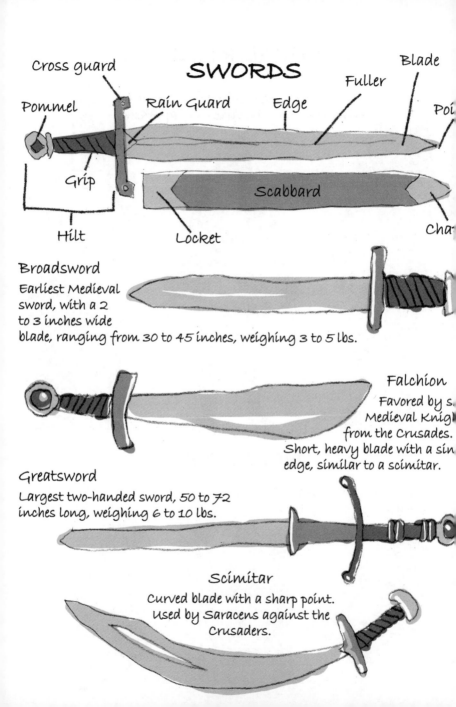

SWORDS

Cross guard
Pommel
Rain Guard
Edge
Fuller
Blade
Poi[nt]
Grip
Scabbard
Hilt
Locket
Cha[pe]

Broadsword
Earliest Medieval sword, with a 2 to 3 inches wide blade, ranging from 30 to 45 inches, weighing 3 to 5 lbs.

Falchion
Favored by s[ome] Medieval Knig[hts] from the Crusades. Short, heavy blade with a sin[gle] edge, similar to a scimitar.

Greatsword
Largest two-handed sword, 50 to 72 inches long, weighing 6 to 10 lbs.

Scimitar
Curved blade with a sharp point. Used by Saracens against the Crusaders.

WEAPONS

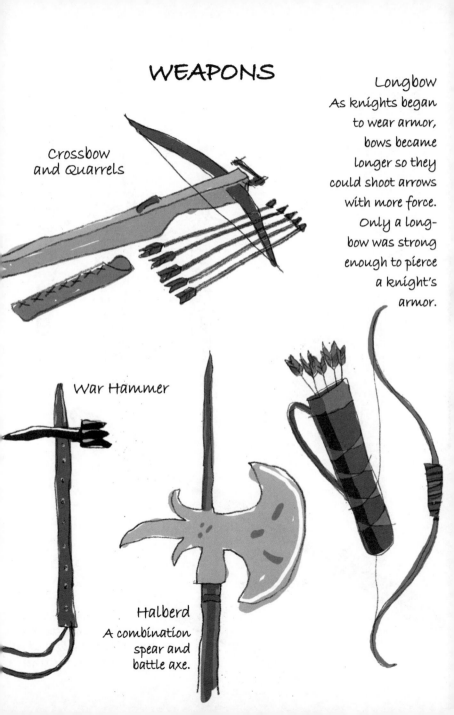

Crossbow
and Quarrels

Longbow
As knights began
to wear armor,
bows became
longer so they
could shoot arrows
with more force.
Only a long-
bow was strong
enough to pierce
a knight's
armor.

War Hammer

Halberd
A combination
spear and
battle axe.

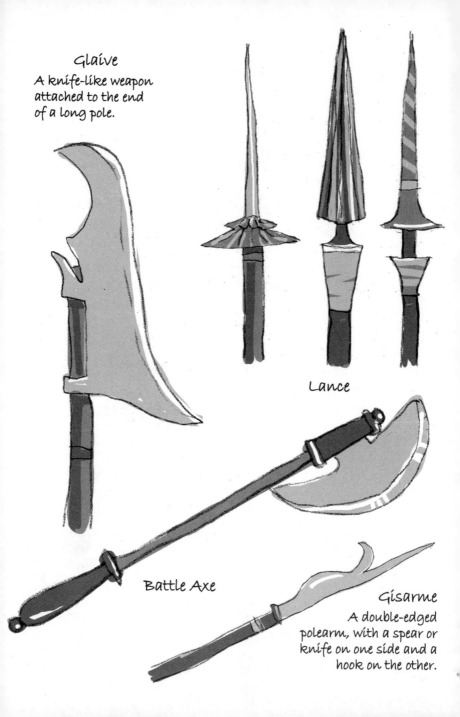

Glaive
A knife-like weapon attached to the end of a long pole.

Lance

Battle Axe

Gisarme
A double-edged polearm, with a spear or knife on one side and a hook on the other.

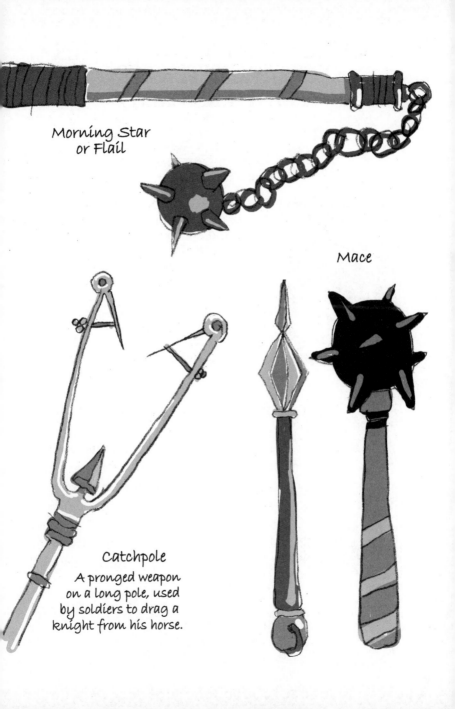

Morning Star
or Flail

Mace

Catchpole

A pronged weapon
on a long pole, used
by soldiers to drag a
knight from his horse.

CHECK OUT THESE OTHER *EXCITING* TITLES FROM FLINDERS PRESS!

 **BENJAMIN FLINDERS'** father carved him a wooden sword out of a tree branch when Ben was just a small boy. With the aide of his best friend, Sir John, he bravely defended his castle (the neighbor's overgrown bushes)from attacks by his younger brothers, Squire Scott and Squire Timothy. Now he spins tales of adventure to his own children at their home in Los Angeles, California.

 **NICOLAUS SERR** got his start riding horses while in search of a fair maiden during his college days. There he was knighted "Serr (pronounced "Sir") Nicolaus" by his close friends. Little did he know how relevant this nickname would become until he was commissioned to illustrate this book. He still dreams of finding a beautiful damsel (hopefully not in a whole lot of distress) and settling down in his castle in Salt Lake City, Utah.